"You're so beautiful."

Tyler couldn't take his eyes off Libby.

She blushed. "I think the coffee has affected your brain."

He shook his head. "No, I thought you were beautiful the first time I saw you. I know this sounds weird, but I look at you and I feel as if I've known you all my life."

"Be careful, Tyler. I suspect you might have a romantic soul."

"I think I was supposed to meet up with you, Lib."

Libby got up and walked around to him. Tyler spun in his chair to face her as she stood in front of him. She combed her fingers through his hair, pushing the unruly waves from his forehead. He kept his eyes on her face as he lifted his hands to hers.

"Maybe it's magic in the air. Maybe it's Christmas. Maybe it's a virus," she said.

He grinned and stood. "I'll go with the magic." His eyes darkened with desire, and he lowered his lips to hers.

Dear Reader,

Christmas is one of those magical seasons when the world is made up of twinkling lights on houses, candy canes and waving Santas in the front yard and the scent of pine all through the house. What child can resist this time of year? In fact, what adult can resist it, too?

Our neighborhood likes to decorate, and there even seems to be a friendly rivalry as to who gets more creative each year. One night during the season, we're out there to greet Santa when he rides down the street on top of an antique fire engine. Even our dog, Bogie, gets into the season with his red-and-white sweater.

Obviously I love Christmas, but what prompted me to write this particular Christmas story? Well, do you remember times as a child when you would be angry at your parents and you'd tell them that they'd be really unhappy if you weren't around? Then you might have packed up a few of your things and prepared to leave home. I know I did it. I made it as far as the corner, then I went back home and asked my dad to drive me since it was getting dark. Do you remember if you ever tried this around the holiday season?

Libby Barnes, for very personal reasons, has this problem where she doesn't want to be around any of her family. Unfortunately, guardian angel Matthias (whom you may remember from some of my other books) takes that wish to the extreme!

Family and friends are important all year-round, but there's always something special about the Christmas holidays that makes them even more important. We all know that—and now Libby is about to learn it, too.

So, enjoy a glass of eggnog and a piece of my special pumpkin cheesecake and please, have a wonderful holiday season!

Linda Randell Wisdom

Linda Randall Wisdom

BELLS, RINGS & ANGELS' WINGS

Harlequin Books

TORONTO • NEW YORK • LONDON
AMSTERDAM • PARIS • SYDNEY • HAMBURG
STOCKHOLM • ATHENS • TOKYO • MILAN
MADRID • WARSAW • BUDAPEST • AUCKLAND

Many thanks to my husband, Bob,
for rescuing a smashed disk and somehow coaxing life
out of it. And more thanks to Debra Matteucci, for
having the patience of a saint.

ISBN 0-373-16707-5

BELLS, RINGS & ANGELS' WINGS

Prologue

"Surely you can't expect me to take on another job of that magnitude. Not after I was given the impression that the Brianne situation would be my last assignment."

"Nothing of the sort was stated at the time, Matthias. That is just wishful thinking on your part. It has been known for some time you have hoped for a seat on the Council of Elders."

Matthias was incapable of hate, but he could gather up feelings of disdain toward Lucius. The man could be so smug at times! He had turned even worse since he'd become a member of the council. He seemed to enjoy the fact he was on it and Matthias was not.

"While your work with Allie Walker and Brianne Sinclair was successful, we felt your methods were unorthodox, to say the least," Simon, the head of the council, gently chided Matthias. "Still, as you said, it was successful."

Pride was not permitted among their kind, but Matthias felt it nonetheless.

"That is why we are asking you to take on this very special assignment."

A parchment filled with strange symbols appeared in the air and drifted toward Matthias. A quick scan told him all he needed to know about its content.

"This has to be accomplished during the Christmas holidays." He made it sound like a curse.

"Yes, it does."

"Does this mean I will have to deal with Santa Claus again?" He felt panic inside. "The last time we were forced together was not pleasant. I'd rather work with that blasted Easter Bunny!"

"I'm sure that could be arranged," Lucius said with a sly smile.

Matthias tamped down his instinctive retort. It would not do to anger the elders when he so badly wanted to be one of them.

He studied the parchment again.

"She is very important to the future, Matthias," Simon explained. "Her progeny will give the world a great scientist in the next century. It is our duty to make sure nothing goes wrong."

"She is a very unhappy woman," Matthias said after he finished reading the report.

"Yes, she is, but we are certain you will do

whatever is necessary to bring her soul back to where it belongs.''

Matthias left the council chambers with a heavy heart and more than a little pique in his spirit.

''If that's the way they feel, then I will just have to somehow turn this horrible disaster around,'' he grumbled to himself as he made his way to the transportation chamber. ''And here I thought I would not have to return to Earth again! As far as I am concerned, this will be the last time.''

With a heavy sigh, he entered the chamber and set the coordinates for his destination.

''Willow Hills, Indiana,'' he muttered. ''And to think I once called Babylon barbaric!''

Chapter One

"Can you believe it? I swear you barely finish celebrating Labor Day and the stores are already stocking Halloween costumes and candy. Then when that is barely over, a body has to start thinking about Thanksgiving. Next thing you know Christmas decorations will be on the shelves." Maude Chester babbled on as she took each item out of the basket and ran it along the infrared scanner. The total showed up on the register screen. "Here we go, hon—forty-three eighty-six." She leaned closer to study her customer. "You better not be on a diet, Libby Barnes, because I swear a breath of wind could blow you away now."

Libby stretched her lips in a smile that felt as false as she was sure it looked.

"With all the layers I'm wearing today I'm surprised you can see more than my face," she commented, using her ATM card to pay for the groceries.

Maude nodded. "I can see enough of you to tell you're not eating properly. That boy should be filling you up with good food. You'll need some insulation for winter."

Libby smiled and shook her head.

"You worry too much, Maude." She pushed the cart out of the store and into the parking lot. Even though she was out of earshot, she could easily guess what Maude was saying to the next customer.

Poor Libby, losing a child the way she did. The little girl was only a few months old, too. Libby never did get over it. And if you look at that handsome husband of hers you can tell it's been just as rough on him. Such a lovely couple. She really needs to think about having another baby instead of spending so much time at the cemetery the way she does. Watching over her dead baby won't bring that little darling back....

Libby chanced a quick look over her shoulder. Maude was talking fast and furiously to Mrs. Anders, and from the sad expressions on their faces she knew she was right. She was the focus of their conversation.

"Gossipy old biddies." She unlocked the trunk of her Honda and placed the grocery bags inside.

"You'd think they'd have better things to do than plan other people's lives."

Libby wrapped her jacket more tightly around her as she climbed into her car. For a moment, her eyes focused on the small portrait hanging from the rearview mirror. The clear plastic rectangle swung gently to and fro. A tiny face with rosebud lips looked back at her. The baby's face was pink, with minuscule eyes scrunched up as if sleep was the most important part of her life. Doll-like fists bunched up by her chin.

She never had a chance.

Libby took a deep breath and started up the car. She smiled and waved at anyone who waved at her and made her way out of the parking lot as quickly as possible.

She wasn't comfortable in public now. Where once she'd enjoyed going out and being with her friends, she now went out only when it was absolutely necessary. She preferred the quiet of the house, where she could be alone with her thoughts. Where she could reflect on the events of the past year that had shaped her life. A life some said was no life at all.

She'd taken a leave of absence from her job as a preschool teacher. Looking at faces of little girls would have been too painful for her when her own daughter would never have a chance to grow up. It was easier to stay home and think of how things might have been.

She drove into the garage and climbed out. Carrying a bag in each arm, she stepped into the kitchen. The warmth of the room was welcome after the frigid air outside.

"And what have you been up to while I was gone?" she asked as she set the bags on the counter. A fluffy black cat with brilliant green eyes looked up and purred his reply with haughty disdain, as if he hated being disturbed by a mere human.

"No, Khan, I didn't forget your food," she told the cat as she emptied the bags and took off her coat, draping it over the back of a chair. "And as soon as I put the roast in the oven, I'll feed you. I promise."

Her movements were sure and easy as she assembled the ingredients for dinner. Not one motion was wasted during her work. She could have been a well-tuned robot.

HOW LONG HAD IT BEEN since he had come home to hear music and laughter ringing throughout the house? How many times had he driven home wondering what he'd walk in and find? Would it be classical music or rock and roll greeting him? Would Libby welcome him with a deep curtsy or entice him into a jitterbug? It never mattered, because he loved all the facets that made up Libby Bennett Barnes.

Now Tyler could only pray as he walked inside their home. No music today. All he heard was the muted sounds of pots and pans clattering on the stove and Libby periodically saying something to the cat.

The laughter and music were gone. When their daughter died, Tyler felt as if Libby had died with her.

He took a deep breath as he hung his jacket in the closet and unlaced his work boots.

"Hey, what are you doing in there? Burning old, moldy clothes?" he bellowed, in hopes of getting a rise out of her.

"That's not funny, Tyler."

His mouth turned downward. Close, but not close enough. He thought about the past, when the old Libby would have bantered back with a description of roasting his jeans, and how his socks would make a lovely piecrust.

Their jokes had disappeared with the music and laughter. The woman with the sunny nature was gone, replaced by a wan creature who treated mirth like a sin. Happiness simply wasn't allowed. That part of her had been gone since...

Pain radiated through him like a hot knife as memories swamped him. Fast-moving images of Libby holding up the baby.

Of many evenings they had been content to just stand by the crib and watch her sleep. Of the times they'd lie in bed with Sara bundled up between them and laughingly plan her future.

She'll find a new galaxy out there. Or she'll be the first woman president. Then they'd say there was no reason why she couldn't do both!

Then came the morning when Libby went into the nursery to get her up and their little angel's eyes didn't open. And never would. Libby's screams still lived in his mind.

Tyler went into the bathroom to wash up for dinner.

"I made a stew," Libby said by way of greeting when he walked into the kitchen.

"It smells good." Tyler secretly hated himself for mouthing clichés instead of just coming out and saying what he wanted to say.

He wanted to yell at Libby and shake her out of the cocoon she'd wrapped herself up in. He wanted his wife back, the woman he'd fallen in love with. He wanted her to remember that he hurt, too. At times he had hurt so much he didn't think he could go on. But after a while, he'd told himself that they had to get on with the business of living. Their lives hadn't stopped when little Sara's heart stopped beating. The only trouble was, Tyler was having trouble convincing Libby of that. She seemed to remain in limbo.

"How was your day?" he asked, reaching into the refrigerator and pulling out a bottle of beer. He snapped off the cap and drank thirstily.

"Nothing special." She didn't look at him as she replied.

Tyler thought about times when she'd regaled him with stories about her students, or later on, with everything new Sara had done that day.

"It looks like we'll get the contract for the new high school," he told her with forced enthusiasm as he pulled bowls and silverware out of cabinets and drawers.

From the day they were first married, they'd shared housekeeping chores. He set the bowls, one a bright turquoise and the other a deep rose-pink, on the table. He remembered how much he'd teased her when she'd talked him into buying the brightly colored Fiesta ware. She told him that the festive-looking dinnerware would make their meals seem like a party. And if there was something the old Libby could do it was make any meal of the day seem like a party.

He missed those times.

"They're going to build it over on Waverly, where Ray's hardware store used to be."

Libby nodded as she ladled stew into the two bowls and set a covered basket of warm French bread on the table.

"I guess that must make Fred happy," she

murmured. Fred was Tyler's boss, the owner of the construction firm Tyler worked for.

"There's work we can do before the snow comes," he replied, digging into the stew. "I also want to finish insulating the attic before the weather gets too cold. Frank and Harvey said they'd come over and help."

Libby nodded and just continued to eat, taking tiny bites of her food.

Tyler swallowed a sigh. They had bought the house more than a year ago, when Libby's belly was softly rounded and they were looking at a future bright with promise. The house was more expensive than their budget had allowed for, and a fixer-upper to boot, but they hadn't minded. Where some might have seen a two-story clunker complete with a leaky basement, Libby and Tyler visualized the large backyard filled with shiny, new playground equipment and children running all through the spacious house.

Now, most of the rooms sported either new paint or wallpaper on the walls, but the only room that was completely finished was one with a door firmly closed and rarely opened. It didn't matter. Tyler could envision its content perfectly.

A lovely white crib with a Bugs Bunny mobile hanging overhead. A large, cream-colored teddy bear sat in a corner of the crib. Beneath him the mattress was covered with a bright yellow, pink, blue and green woven blanket. Nearby stood the changing table, decorated with the same brightly colored border wallpaper as the walls. A teddy bear night-light that doubled as a music box lay on a small white table near the crib to keep all the bad dreams away.

It was the first room they had furnished after they moved in. Libby had wanted the nursery ready for its occupant the moment she came home from the hospital. No matter if their own bedroom was a nightmare of purple wallpaper that belonged in a carnival fun house or the living room walls were painted a dark brown that Libby used to joke made them look like the inside of a mud hut. The nursery took priority.

A lump the size of Alaska settled in Tyler's throat. He set his spoon down and took a swallow of beer in hopes of drowning that lump.

"I saw Marie today. She wants us to come over Saturday for dinner. She's already planning Thanksgiving dinner," he commented. "She also said you haven't called her recently."

Libby didn't look up from her food. "I've been busy."

"Too busy to talk to your mother? The woman you've always talked to on a daily basis? What are you too busy doing, Libby? Sitting in this house, refusing to talk to anyone, just sitting in the silence."

Her eyes glimmered with tears as she looked up at him. "Why should I leave the house? There's nothing out there for me. Everything worthwhile I had is gone."

Tyler battled the pain gnawing his insides.

"And what the hell am I?" he asked in a dangerously quiet voice.

Whatever tears had threatened to fall from her eyes were gone as she stared at him without a speck of emotion on her face. "Just a man who no longer cares that his daughter is dead."

Tyler's appetite disappeared, leaving behind a cold anger. "Oh, I care that my daughter is dead and lies up in that cemetery alone with no one to keep her warm. And I care that she'll never grow up and have friends or go to the prom or get married," he stated in a cold, hard voice. "But Sara's gone and there's nothing I can do about it. I can only go on. The thing is, I've managed to go on and you haven't." His features were set in a tight mask. "The way things are between us, I might as well have buried you up there with her."

Libby's eyes were dark in her face as she stared at him. "You have no idea how I feel," she said in a low voice throbbing with fury and pain. "You weren't the one to go into the nursery and find her lying there." Her voice rose as she stood up. "She never had a chance!"

"Stop it!" Tyler jumped out of his chair and

took hold of Lily's shoulders, giving her a hard shake. Her head bobbed back and forth loosely. "Just stop it, Libby!"

She carefully disengaged herself from his hold and stepped back. She didn't say one word as she left the kitchen.

Tyler slumped in his chair. He felt closer to eighty than thirty.

He had planned to tell Libby it looked as if another dream was about to come true. Fred was talking about taking on a partner, and he was willing to allow Tyler to work his way into the partnership. He wanted to talk to her about trying to have another child. He refused to believe that God would take away another baby from them.

He looked upward. "You wouldn't, would you?" he whispered. "Please, help her see that we have so much ahead of us. I don't want to go on without her. I love her too much."

Tyler's shoulders rose and fell in a resigned sigh. He could only hope someone had heard him. Was wanting his wife back asking too much?

LIBBY WAS USED TO LOSING track of time by now. When she woke up the next morning, Tyler had already left for work. All she found was an indentation on the pillow next to hers and a pile of wet towels on the bathroom counter. When the phone rang, she rolled over and muttered a half-sleepy hello.

"Elizabeth Louise, in case you've forgotten who this is, I am your mother," a firm voice announced over the line. "I am the woman who raised you and fed brownies to all those boys hanging around our house for so many years. The least you could do is call me more than once a year."

"I talked to you the day before yesterday," Libby corrected.

"The last time you talked to me was last Tuesday which is more than a week ago." Marie Bennett's voice softened. "You have to stop this, baby."

"Stop what?" Libby asked, feigning ignorance.

"You know very well what I'm talking about. It's been long enough. You need to go on, dear. I miss my daughter and I want my little girl back."

Libby hardened her heart against the sorrow in her mother's voice.

"I'd like my little girl back, too, Mom, but it just isn't possible for me. Why do you feel you should have all the luck?"

Libby could hear the older woman's deep sigh at her own deliberate cruelty.

"You can't turn bitter from all this, Libby. It

isn't good and it won't make things any better for you," she said quietly. "All it will accomplish is pushing away your husband and your family. Is that what you truly want?"

"What I want is my daughter back. Since that isn't possible, I guess I'll just have to settle for what I can have."

"Then think about this, Elizabeth. The holidays are coming and the last thing I want is for you to stray from us at this time."

Holidays. Libby's heart felt as if it were free-falling in space.

Her family were big believers in celebrating the holidays, and each holiday was turned into a big party that usually included most of the town. From Halloween to New Years it seemed the family never stopped celebrating. This was to have been her daughter's introduction to the holidays, Bennett-Barnes style.

A tiny pumpkin costume for Halloween, lovingly stitched by Libby, was now packed away in the cedar chest in the nursery, along with a length of forest green velvet and creamy white lace meant for a Christmas dress. They would never be used.

"Are you sure it's proper to celebrate?"

"Yes, Libby, it is. Darling, we all hate it that she's gone, but we have to go on. *You* have to go on. You and Tyler were blessed once. You can be again.''

Libby sat up in bed. ''What if it happens again? What if we have another child who doesn't wake up one morning? I won't take that chance.''

''Sweetheart, if you think like that, you will only keep burying your head in the sand so nothing bad will happen to you again. I'm sorry you had to suffer such a loss, but you are not the only one who has gone through this and you won't be the last. Sara wouldn't want you to wall yourself off from everyone, including your husband. Don't punish Tyler for what happened, dear. And don't punish yourself.''

''No lecture, Mom, please?'' Libby took a deep breath for fear she was going to cry. ''I'm sorry, I have to go.'' She carefully replaced the receiver and flopped back against the pillows. She felt wearier than when she'd gone to sleep the night before.

Finally, she dragged herself out of bed and pulled out a pair of jeans and a dark gray sweatshirt.

Is there some reason why you cannot choose clothing that is a little more cheerful? Right now, you look as if you are preparing to blend in with a dark corner. And I must say you do it beautifully.

''What?'' Libby spun around, fearfully expecting to face whoever had spoken to her. But she saw no one.

"Wonderful, now you're hearing voices," she murmured to herself as she went into the bathroom to wash her face and brush her hair. "If the family knew, they'd probably try to send me to that psychologist again."

When Libby heard the telephone ring this time, she was more cautious in answering it.

"If you are lying in bed playing lady of the manor I will hate you."

Libby's lips curved in a semblance of a smile at the sound of her younger sister's chirpy voice. "Why? Because you decided to take an eight o'clock class this semester?"

"Hey, if you saw the instructor, you'd understand why," Vicki Bennett retorted.

"I'll be curious to see your grades from that class at the end of the semester."

"All right, you've done your best to see if I'm the perfect student and I am, but I have no classes today and I want to go shopping with my favorite older sister. I'll even treat you to lunch."

"Vicki, I'm your only older sister," Libby said dryly.

"And that's why you're my favorite. So do whatever you need to do to get ready and I'll pick you up in a half hour. Uh-uh," she said quickly, anticipating her sister's protest. "No excuses, Lib.

We're going to spend money today.'' She hung up without letting Libby get another word in.

A day out with your sister is a wonderful idea. Do make sure you buy yourself something more cheerful to wear than that dreary thing you have on now. I am certain you will want to change your clothes before you leave the house.

Libby looked warily around in search of the source of the slightly sarcastic voice, even though it seemed to come from inside her head.

''Maybe I do need a day out.''

By the time Vicki drove up in her sporty red Honda Prelude, Libby had changed into a pair of black wool pants and a black-and-cream, marled-yarn sweater in deference to the cool weather.

''What's the occasion?'' She asked, settling herself in the passenger seat. ''You never offer to buy anyone lunch. You're usually trying to mooch off the rest of us. You already know I won't do your homework for you.''

''I am truly hurt. I want to do a good deed and spend some quality time with my sister and all you can do is suspect me of something.'' Vicki merrily swung her car into traffic, blithely disregarding any car that might be in her way.

Twenty minutes later she was parking in the mall's garage.

''I could get more excited about winter clothes

if we didn't have to wear so many layers to stay warm,'' she confided, pausing to study a store's window display. ''How can you attract a guy when you're wearing thermal underwear under four sweaters and a parka?''

''The first time I met Tyler I was wearing a playsuit that made me look like the Pillsbury Doughboy,'' Libby said. ''He didn't seem to mind.''

Vicki gave her a long-suffering look. ''You were four years old and he was six. Plus he thought you were hot stuff because you shared your brownie with him. What little boy is going to turn down a brownie?''

''Point taken,'' Libby conceded. She walked toward one of the stores and stared at a display of baby clothing in the window. She stood mesmerized by a tiny knit sweater until Vicki grabbed her arm and dragged her away.

''There's a dance on campus next week and I intend to buy a killer dress,'' she explained, heading down the mall. ''You're just the person to help me find it.''

Libby had forgotten how exhausting shopping with Vicki could be. The young woman tried on every dress the various stores had to offer, and somehow still found time to bully Libby into trying on a few things. She even managed to talk her into purchasing a couple of sweaters and a blouse.

"Maybe we should see if any of the cosmetic counters are doing makeovers," Vicki mused as she stopped to study a pair of strappy, high-heeled sandals. "You need a new shade of lipstick or something. You looked better when you had the flu two years ago."

"Thank you so much for the compliment."

"You always look so pale now." Vicki wrinkled her nose as she studied her sister, whose only concession to makeup was a pale pink lipstick and a hint of mascara. "This just will not do."

She grabbed Libby's arm and pulled her along. "Come on, elderly sister of mine, I intend to see you looking gorgeous when we leave here."

"Vicki!" Libby's protest was ignored as her sibling marched to the cosmetics department like a woman on a mission.

Chapter Two

"I can't believe how lucky I got today in finding everything I wanted," Vicki crowed as they drove home late that afternoon. "I was so glad that dress was on sale. Otherwise, I wouldn't have been able to get those shoes."

"True, you couldn't have lived without the shoes," Libby murmured. She glanced at her reflection in the mirror attached to the sun visor. The deep coral lipstick, smoky green eye shadow and matching liner, and tawny blush looked garish to her. It had been some time since she had bothered with makeup. She never felt as if she had the energy or inclination for the time it took to add color to her cheeks and lips.

Except for that brief moment in front of the children's clothing store, she hadn't thought of her baby once all afternoon. Pain sliced through her body. She could feel the moisture gathering at the corners of her eyes and a tight sensation low in her belly. How could she forget so easily?

"Don't!" There was a sharpness in Vicki's voice that hadn't been there before. "We had a fun day out and I'm not going to let you ruin it."

Libby ordinarily would have snapped back at her, but her gaze was fixed on the fifth house from the corner of the street Vicki had turned down on. Her house. A blue Explorer and black pickup truck were parked in the driveway. The back door of the Explorer was open, revealing several boxes. More boxes were piled in the back of the pickup, along with pieces of furniture.

"Let me out," she ordered, grabbing hold of the door handle.

Vicki grasped her arm as she slowed the car.

Libby whipped her head around and stared at her sister with a look so fierce the younger woman recoiled from her.

"We only wanted to help," she whispered.

"If you want to help, stay out of my life." Libby pushed open the door and climbed out so fast she stumbled and almost fell on the road. She quickly regained her balance and ran down the sidewalk to her house. She pushed the front door open and ran in, deliberately ignoring her sister's pleas as she started toward the back of the house, where she could hear voices.

The room was now empty of furniture, with the

exception of a few half-filled boxes placed near the door. Libby's mother was in the midst of carefully wrapping the bear night-light in paper and placing it in a box. Tyler, bent over sealing a box with packing tape, had his back to Libby.

"I guess this is it," he said.

Marie Bennett looked up and saw Libby standing in the doorway. "Tyler," she murmured in warning.

He turned and stared at his wife.

"What do you think you're doing?" Libby demanded in a low voice, advancing on them.

"It had to be done, sweetheart," he said, reaching out to restrain her. "We knew how difficult it would be for you, so Marie came over to help me."

Libby shook off his hand as if it was something disgusting. "You had no right!"

"Elizabeth, you can no longer live in the past. You need to go forward," her mother said firmly. "Don't wall yourself off from having more children. You and Tyler deserve a large family. That's what the two of you have always wanted."

"Why? So we can go through this pain again?" Libby asked, her voice rising in pitch. "So I have two graves to visit instead of one?"

"Stop it, Libby!" Tyler spoke in a low, firm voice. "We all hurt from this and all you've done is allow the pain to fester. I love you and I can't allow you to keep on this way."

Libby shook her head as she slowly backed away from him.

"Why are you doing this, Tyler?" she asked in a little-girl voice filled with pain. "You know how important she was to me. How I loved her."

His face was also filled with pain and sorrow, but something else was there that tore at Libby.

Pity. For her.

"Don't look at me like that!" she snapped. "You all act as if I've lost my wits. Well, I haven't. There is no set mourning period in the rule books. In some cultures, you can mourn forever. I will not forget my child!"

"Then why won't you say her name?" He stepped closer to her. "All you ever say is 'my baby,' 'our baby,' but you never say her name."

Horror crossed her face as his words sunk in. "How can you be so cruel?" she whispered. "Her name is engraved in my heart."

"Honey, it may feel cruel now, but the time will come when you'll understand." Marie moved forward, her arms outstretched to embrace her daughter.

Libby backed up even more. "Why can't you just let me handle this myself?" She kept backing up until she stood in the doorway.

"Because you aren't handling it," Tyler replied.

She shook her head. "I am handling it. It's the rest of you who aren't." She spun around and ran out of the house.

"Libby!" He started after her, but Marie grabbed hold of his arm.

"Let her go, Tyler," she said softly. "She needs to be alone and think all this through. Once she's had a chance to consider everything she'll realize we did this for her. That we only wanted to spare her any more pain." She patted his arm and moved away to seal the last box. "Vicki, would you take this out to the truck for me, please?" She handed it to her other daughter, then stood up on her toes and pressed a kiss against Tyler's cheek. "We'll see you Saturday night, dear."

After they had gone, he stood in the now empty room, listening to the sound of the front door closing. He remembered the pain etched on Libby's face as she'd realized he and her mother had cleared out the nursery.

"She's my first and last love," he said out loud. "From that first time I saw Libby dressed in a pink snowsuit, her hair pulled back in braids, I knew I was going to marry her when I grew up. As far as I was concerned, there wasn't anyone else. She was the first girl I ever kissed, my first lover. I don't want to lose her.''

He glanced at the clock to check the time. No matter what his mother-in-law had said about leaving Libby alone, he was only going to give her another half hour before going out to look for her. Knowing Libby as well as he did, he figured she was at the park a few blocks away.

He had an idea tonight they were going to have the fight they'd never had. But maybe it was for the best if he wanted to get his old Libby back.

LIBBY WAS INDEED at the park, with her coat buttoned all the way up to her chin to ward off the cold, although she was so angry she really didn't feel the chill. She sat in a swing, using her foot to push it back and forth.

''Why can't they leave me alone?'' she muttered. Why did everyone have to tell her how she was supposed to lead her life?

It might have something to do with their loving you so much.

Her head whipped one way, then the other to find the source of the voice—the same one she had heard that morning.

''I refuse to believe there's a voice talking to me inside my head.''

I am not exactly talking to you inside your head. Oh, my, you women are difficult.

Libby stilled. "All right, what's the joke?"

A heavy sigh preceded the next statement. *There is no joke. I have been sent here to help you. From what I have seen so far, my dear, you need a great deal of assistance.*

She looked around, but could see nothing in the twilight. Not a shadow of a person standing nearby. She was alone in the park. There weren't even any bushes nearby that could hide someone who might want to play a cruel trick on her.

"Fine, my imagination has decided to take a vacation and fly to la la land," she said. "Now I'm talking to an invisible man."

What I am is an entity sent to help you.

"Which is probably another word for a doctor sent by my parents or my husband," she muttered, pumping her legs back and forth to get the swing going.

I am here strictly for you. The deep sigh was heard again. *Women are so difficult to deal with. The last woman I assisted was positive I was from outer space. I blame the media for all these fantasies.*

"Oh, I get it. You're my guardian angel. How comforting that thought is. It's a good thing I'm out here alone so no one can see me talking to myself."

No, angels are another department entirely. I am someone who only comes to help when it ap-

pears there is no other recourse for that mortal. And you, my dear Libby, definitely fit in that category.

"Then why don't you just show yourself, wave your wand or whatever and leave me do with my life as I wish?" At that moment, she felt a hand planted against her back pushing her forward. The swing swept upward. "All right! All right!" She put her feet down to stop the swing, skidding slightly in the dirt. "If you're not a figment of my imagination, you'll show yourself to me."

Materializing is not a part of my job description.

Libby smiled in triumph. "Then you're not real. And I would say in about ten minutes Tyler will come over here, tell me he's sorry for what he's done and that he wants me to come back to the house with him."

And what do you want?

Libby took a deep breath. Perhaps talking to herself wasn't so bad, after all. She could say what she wanted out loud and there was no one to censor her thoughts. She might even feel better after she'd gotten it out of her system.

"I want them to leave me alone. I want them to stop pretending Sara doesn't exist any longer. I want to live my own life without them telling me what's good for me," she stated.

That sounds like something an adolescent would say in order to have his or her own way.

She shook her head. "No, it's just that they don't realize how important Sara was to me, and I can't give her up just because they tell me to."

What about Tyler? Is he not also important to you?

Libby felt a pang in the vicinity of her heart. "He's very important to me," she said softly. "But Sara was a wonderful part of both of us. She had my eyes and Tyler's grin. And we had such plans for her."

And now you're angry at the world because she was taken away from you.

Libby straightened up at that statement. "Yes, I am," she admitted. "It wasn't fair that she died."

And you'd be happier if they all left you alone so you could grieve for your child in peace.

Libby took a deep breath. "Yes."

The moment she spoke, a cold wind sliced through her and she could see flurries of white drift around her.

"There wasn't anything in the weather reports about snow tonight," she murmured, tucking her hands in her coat pockets.

Perhaps it would be a good time for you to return home.

Libby pushed herself out of the swing and

stood up. As she walked out of the park, she noticed the snow flurries were getting heavier, as if they were trying to wrap themselves around her. She was grateful for her heavy coat as she reached the sidewalk.

"You'd think Tyler would see the snow falling and drive down to pick me up," she grumbled, ducking her head. "He had to have known I'd be here."

Considering the way you've been behaving lately, you should be grateful he is even willing to speak to you.

"There's nothing worse than a smart-ass voice," she practically snarled.

Amazing. My last subject called me a voice with an attitude. Pride filled his words.

"I can see why." She reached the end of her block and started up it. The streetlights had just come on to battle the early evening darkness. "I can't believe how quickly this began. If it keeps up, the snowplows will have to come out to clear the streets."

Perhaps. Perhaps not.

"Riddles. Now he gives me riddles." Libby slowed her steps as she approached the house she thought was hers. It was hers, wasn't it? Yes, the right numbers were painted on the exterior by the front door, but even in the dim light she could see the color wasn't the same pale green she and Tyler had painted it a year ago.

Why was her house now dark blue with gray trim? Whose motorcycle was in the driveway? And why all that loud music? She punched the doorbell once, then several times more. The moment the door opened, she wished she hadn't been so eager to get inside. The man standing before her wore tight jeans that couldn't contain the belly hanging over it. His leather vest, worn with no shirt underneath, displayed the variety of tattoos dappling his forearms.

"Hey there, gorgeous, you here for the party?" He leered at her as he held up a beer can in a hand the size of a small ham.

Libby couldn't stop staring back. Behind him, she could see a small crowd of men and women all drinking and dancing. She didn't recognize any of them. She shook her head and backed away.

"Well, hell, come on in!" he boomed, waving his beer can around. "The more the merrier."

"No," she whispered, still backing away.

Come along, Libby.

"What's wrong?" she whispered, once she reached the street.

Put your hand in your right pocket.

Libby did as she was told. Her fingers closed around cold metal, its sharp edges digging into her skin. She pulled it out and saw it was a key with a plastic tag hanging from it.

"This is from the Willow Hills Motel," she murmured.

I suggest you pick up your pace, so you can return to your room before it gets much colder.

"My room? Why do I have a motel key in my pocket? Where's Tyler? Why are all those strangers in my house? Why is it a different color? Where are all my flowers?" she asked in a lost-little-girl voice.

Go to the motel, Libby. I will explain it all when we arrive there. I promise.

Libby felt as if she were walking through cotton wool as she left the house she had thought her own and headed in the direction of the main part of town. Strangely, she didn't feel cold any longer as she walked the many blocks toward the motel. She just put one foot in front of the other and kept on walking.

Your room is at the rear of the motel.

Libby inserted the key in the lock. The door opened to reveal a small room with a neatly made king-size bed. Three suitcases sat on the floor and the bathroom light was on. She slowly stepped inside and closed the door behind her. After her chilly walk, the hot air blasting at her felt welcome. She peeled off her coat and laid it across the chair.

"What is going on?" It wasn't until then that she happened to look down at her left hand. It was bare of any jewelry. She cried out in shock and rubbed her third finger. There wasn't even an indentation in the skin to indicate she had ever worn a ring.

"Where is my ring?" She looked around wildly, as if it would gleam in the darkness to help her find it. "It couldn't have just slipped off!"

Why don't you sit down while I explain this to you.

She sat, but couldn't stop rubbing her bare ring finger.

"Fine, I'm sitting down. Now, if you're not a figment of my imagination, you'll make yourself visible and tell me why my house doesn't look the same and why there were strangers there. And why I'm not wearing my wedding ring." Hysteria rose up inside her.

I am not in the habit of making myself visible just because someone insists upon it.

"I'm this far—" she held her thumb and forefinger up a scant inch apart "—from screaming bloody murder. Let's make it easier for both of us, shall we?"

Libby's first warning that she truly wasn't alone was a wisp of smoke that appeared by the chair. It swirled in odd patterns, then slowly formed into the figure of a man.

He didn't appear very tall, about five foot ten inches or so. Brown hair rimmed his head, although the top was bald. Dark eyes peered at her with the wisdom of the ages. She wasn't sure what she expected an "entity" to wear, but black pants and a black turtleneck wasn't it. His arms were crossed in front of his chest.

"Well?" he asked.

For a moment she couldn't speak.

"It's happened. I've gone and lost my mind," she murmured. "You're not real. None of this is real. It's all an ugly dream."

"Oh, I'm real, all right." He picked up her coat, shook it out, then hung it in the closet. He returned to the chair and sat down, carefully adjusting the crease in his pants. "My name is Matthias."

"Matthias," Libby repeated numbly. She couldn't take her eyes off him. "What are you?"

He heaved a deep sigh. "I already explained to you, I am an entity. I am here to help you deal with your sorrow so you can go on with your life."

"Then why the changes with my house?" she demanded. "Where's Tyler? Why am I not wearing my wedding ring?"

Matthias sat back in the chair with his fingers pressed together in steeple fashion.

"Your ring no longer exists. Tyler as your husband doesn't exist, and your house is no longer yours. And, since Tyler is not your husband, he is living on Grover Avenue in the house his parents left him."

"What do you mean he's living in the house his parents left him? They still live there! And how can you say Tyler isn't my husband?"

He shook his head. "They moved to Arizona after his father retired."

"That can't be," she protested. "His father retired and they stayed because they wanted to be here for the baby."

"Things have changed, Libby," Matthias explained in a patient voice.

She looked around the small room. "Such as my being in this motel room for some reason and not in my own house? Tyler's gone, my ring is gone. My life is gone. Now you're here to tell me what's going on. But you're not my guardian angel."

He nodded. "That is correct. I merely guide you when you need guidance."

"Fine. Then tell me why am I here and why my husband is somewhere else?"

"Because in your husband's and your parents' eyes you no longer exist."

Libby froze. "Excuse me?"

Matthias smiled and settled back in the chair, looking proud of his accomplishment.

"It's very simple. You said you did not want them in your life any longer and now they are not. You did not appreciate their interference, so now you are on your own."

Libby was positive the world had started spinning crazily on its axis. She thought about saying something, but nothing came to mind at the moment.

She opted for the only action that seemed reasonable at the moment.

She fell backward unconscious on the bed.

Chapter Three

"It is situations such as this that make me prefer to work with men. At least men do not faint or grow hysterical." A male voice intruded on Libby's fuzzy world. "Well, there *was* that time with Henry VIII, but he was always a trial. The man refused to understand the problem was with him, not with his wives."

"I never get hysterical," Libby said in a weak voice. Her eyes fluttered open and she looked up at Matthias. "And what is this about you knowing Henry VIII? How old are you?"

"Too old for you to figure out," he said smoothly. "Do you feel better now or do you require a glass of water?"

Libby sat up and raised a restraining hand. "No, I'm fine." She paused. "I think." She pressed her fingers against her forehead. She was surprised the skin didn't burn under her touch. She took several deep breaths and discovered her stomach wasn't going to go into upheaval the way she feared it would. She turned her head so she could see Matthias better. "You really knew Henry VIII?"

He rolled his eyes. "It was not one of my better assignments. All the man ever cared about was consuming as much food as he could in one sitting and finding himself a new wife."

The teacher in Libby was fascinated. For a moment she wasn't asking herself the logical question of how the man in front of her could have existed for as many centuries as he implied he had.

"Who else did you meet?" she asked.

He waved his hand in dismissal. "None of my assignments pertain to this case. What matters is you. Now, are you calm enough to listen to me?"

Her expression was wary as she nodded.

Matthias took the chair across from her. As he reached out his hand toward the table beside him, a glass of red wine appeared. He picked it up by its stem, then paused as good manners intruded.

"I apologize for my thoughtlessness. Would you care for some wine?"

She shook her head, amazed. "I think I would be better off with all my wits about me."

He nodded. "Perhaps that would be best." He sipped his wine and studied her with an air of contemplation. "It is natural that you would grieve for your daughter. After all, you had planned for her all your life, hadn't you? When you were seven you had a baby doll you loved to distraction and you announced she looked just like your first child would. You named her Sara. You also assumed you would marry Tyler Barnes when you grew up."

"How did you know all this?" Libby asked in a hushed voice, stunned by his knowledge.

"I read your file before I came down here," he stated as if it were a given. "I know your older brother, Mike, pushed you off your bicycle when you were eight and your arm was broken as a result. Once your arm healed, you got even with him by covering his school project with superglue just before he picked it up. The doctor in the emergency room couldn't stop laughing as he separated Mike's hands from the display. Your parents took away your television privileges for two weeks."

"It would have been a month, but they couldn't stop laughing either, so I got off with two weeks," she murmured, smiling at the memory. She quickly returned to the present. "I still don't understand."

Matthias looked pained. "As I explained, I am here because you have been grieving your daughter's death for so long it has affected your entire family. You are in the process of alienating your husband and your family because you have completely shut them off from your feelings.''

She stiffened. "I always felt a mourning period was appropriate."

"A mourning period cannot be forever. You have to go on with your life, Libby. You need to rediscover the richness you have within yourself."

"And you think I will do this because I no longer have any of my family around me?"

Matthias continued sipping his wine. "That is correct. Isn't that what you wanted, to be alone with your grief? You are here as Libby Douglas. You moved here for a new job. The person you are replacing is going on maternity leave and doesn't plan to return. And please do not worry, you will not be staying in the motel for too long."

Libby closed her eyes in hopes doing so would stop the whirling images dancing inside her brain. It didn't. When she opened them again, she noticed a purse lying on the bed. She didn't remember seeing it there before.

"Mine?" she asked Matthias.

"You will need the proper accessories for your new life."

She picked it up as if it contained a disgusting object and opened it. She pulled out the wallet and studied the contents. All the identification she found stated that she was Elizabeth Douglas.

"How can this be done?" She held up the wallet.

"For us, very easily. I do ask that you go easy on the credit cards. Of course, as long as you're here you will receive the bills." Matthias smiled.

"As long as I'm here," Libby mused. "Oh, I get it! You're just like Clarence."

"Clarence?" He looked puzzled.

"Yes, Clarence. He was the angel in *It's a Wonderful Life*. You know, the movie starring Jimmy Stewart and Donna Reed. Jimmy hates his life and Clarence shows him what the town would be like if he didn't exist. And because Clarence succeeds, he gets his wings. You know that every time a bell rings an angel gets his wings."

Matthias looked heavenward. "Why does everyone use the visual media as an example of how we exist? I will not receive wings for any success. After I finish this assignment I will be entering the Council of Elders, as I deserve."

Libby wrinkled her nose. "Sounds ominous to me."

He looked offended. "On the contrary, it is a very honorable recognition for my work. But first, you need to understand what is expected of you."

"Expected of me?" Libby stared at him. Surely, this was a dream. She probably had fallen off the swing at the park and hit her head. When she came to, Tyler would be holding her and her world would be back to normal.

"This is not a dream, this is the life you wished for," Matthias stated.

Could dream characters read your mind? she wondered.

He offered her a droll look as if he was tired of her trying his patience. "No, I am not a dream and yes, I can read your mind."

"Then what do I have to do to return to my life?" she demanded.

Matthias smiled. "That is for you to find out."

"That's a big help! You told me you were here to guide me."

"Guide you, yes. I'm not here to lead you by the hand."

"And what happens to Tyler during all this?" Saying his name caused an unexpected ache. "Why should he have to go through this, too?"

"I hate to correct you, but he will not be going through anything. He is merely existing in a world without you."

Tyler? Without her? The ache intensified.

Matthias glanced at the small alarm clock set on the bedside table. "It is getting late and you have to report to your new job tomorrow. I suggest you get a good night's rest. I will see you in the morning."

He disappeared as swiftly as he had appeared.

"Wait!" But Libby's protest went unheeded. Her shoulders slumped. While she would have argued with him that she wasn't the least bit tired, she discovered she was feeling weary.

She pushed herself off the bed and walked over to the suitcases. She unzipped the largest one and pushed the cover back.

"These are not my clothes," she murmured, staring at the brightly colored articles.

Yes, they are. Do not worry. You will not find anything in a shade unsuitable for you. And they will be a perfect fit.

She looked around but couldn't see any signs of Matthias.

"But, they're so...bright."

She checked the other two suitcases, digging through the contents until she found a robe and nightgown. She hung up the clothing, amused that wrinkles fell out the moment the garments were placed on a hanger. She also discovered a variety of reading material, including several books she'd planned to read but never managed to find time to.

Libby picked up the robe and a nightgown, then went into the bathroom and turned on the water in the bathtub. She added a few drops of bath oil to the hot water and was soon immersed in the spice-scented water.

"You better not be peeking, Matthias," she called out.

This time there was no answer.

After her bath, she cleansed her face and slipped on her nightgown and robe. By the time she settled herself under the covers, she felt her eyelids drooping and her body relaxing.

"I don't care, it still has to be a dream," she murmured sleepily, curling up on her side. As she fell into a deep sleep, a lone tear gathered at the corner of her eye and silently slipped down her cheek.

LIBBY, YOU HAVE TO wake up. It wouldn't be good form to show up late on your first day of work.

"Don't be mean, Tyler. Let me sleep," she murmured, burrowing under the warm covers. As soon as the words left her mouth she realized the voice she'd heard wasn't her husband's. Then she knew she also wasn't lying in her own bed. She opened one eye to find Matthias sitting in the chair.

"How can I get up?" she asked him. "It's so cold in here I'm likely to turn into a Popsicle." At that instant, she could hear the heater switch on. "Now if you'll just go away for about an hour..." she suggested.

"Of course." In the blink of an eye, he was gone.

Libby took several deep breaths.

"This has to be a dream," she muttered, grabbing her robe and shrugging into it.

Within the appointed hour she showered and put on her makeup. The lipsticks in the cosmetic bag were brighter than she usually wore, but she couldn't fault with how the one she'd chosen looked on her. It wasn't until she had a chance to study her choice of clothing that she felt anger at the entity sent to change her life.

"What is this?" she demanded, holding up a black-and-cream plaid skirt that ended well above her knees. Since there was no answer, she paired the skirt with a red sweater and black opaque tights and black flats. As she studied her reflection in the mirror on the back of the bathroom door, she realized she was dressed the way she used to dress more than a year ago.

"That is much better than those grandmotherly dresses you were wearing," Matthias pronounced as he popped back in.

"Calf-length dresses are in style," she said, refusing to admit she did look better in a shorter skirt. She found red button earrings and a gold chain with an onyx pendant to match the bright red sweater.

"Are you ready for breakfast?"

"Why, are you joining me?"

"Food is not necessary for my existence. But

I will see you again. Here is where you will be working. I'm sure you will have no problem adjusting to your new job." He handed her a piece of paper and disappeared.

"Wonderful. He provides clothes, lodging and a job," Libby murmured as she looked down at the paper. Her face turned white as she read the words.

"No, please," she moaned, dropping onto the end of the bed. If she wanted Matthias to reappear and explain how he could do such a horrible thing to her, she was out of luck. There was only silence. It took her several moments to rouse herself and leave the room.

As Libby stepped outside, a familiar voice sounded inside her head.

The blue Maxima is yours.

"It better have a full tank of gas." She found the keys in her purse and unlocked the driver's door.

Naturally, it has a full tank. I wouldn't give you anything else.

Libby drove to a coffee shop she knew well. At least, one she remembered well. Except she noticed Maxine's now had red-and-white striped awnings in front instead of the homey blue-and-white gingham curtains. Inside was more familiar, with most of the tables and booths filled and waitresses scurrying to fill orders.

Libby's face lit up and she opened her mouth to greet Maxine, the owner, but the woman merely offered her a smile.

"Just one, honey?"

Libby gave her a jerky nod.

"Let's find you a nice table." Maxine led the way toward the rear of the restaurant. She gestured to a chair and handed Libby a menu after she'd sat down. "Would you like coffee?"

Libby nodded and coughed to clear her throat. "Yes, thank you."

"Be right back with your coffee." Maxine took off.

Libby set her purse on an empty chair and opened the menu. As she scanned the offerings, she felt desolate and wondered if she could eat anything at all.

As I explained before, Libby, no one here knows you. You are nothing more than a perfect stranger to them.

That doesn't mean it can't hurt, she thought, positive speaking out loud would only cause unwanted attention.

"Here you go, hon." Maxine set a filled cup in front of her. "Have you decided what you want?"

"I'll have the Belgian waffle with scrambled eggs and bacon," she murmured. "And a large glass of grapefruit juice."

Maxine nodded as she jotted down the order. "You're new around here, aren't you?"

Libby nodded. "I start teaching at Miss Parker's Preschool today."

"That's right, Bonnie is going on maternity leave next week. Well, darlin', if you need anything, you just ask for Maxine." She patted Libby's hand before she rushed off.

Libby could feel her throat close up. *I went to school with her daughter, Karen,* she thought. *I worked here every summer while I was in high school. Maxine was one of the first people to come see me after Sara was gone. And now she doesn't even know me.*

You wanted everyone to leave you in peace, Libby. All I did was grant your wish.

Now she truly understood the adage of being careful what you wished for.

Libby couldn't remember ever coming in here and eating by herself. She always ran into people she knew. She would either share their table or someone would sit down with her, even if it was only to have a cup of coffee or an iced tea.

She glanced around the room and saw many familiar faces. A few looked up and offered her a pleasant, but impersonal, smile. How it hurt that she couldn't walk up and say hello.

But that didn't stop Libby from covertly watching Denise Watkins, who was having breakfast with her fiancé, Carl Lindsay, the manager of the hardware store. She remembered receiving their wedding invitation. She had gone to school with Denise, and years ago they had spent a lot of time together, but Libby couldn't remember the last time she had spoken to her. She'd never even asked her about her wedding plans. And now Denise didn't know her.

Libby pulled a paperback book out of her purse and began reading. She gave Maxine a wan smile when the woman refilled her coffee cup and again when she set her breakfast in front of her.

If I say I wish I'd never made that wish, will my life go back to normal? she asked silently.

No, Libby, it won't. It's too late now.

Are you saying this is a learning experience for me? She didn't bother to hide her sarcasm.

I am a teacher. I am familiar with lessons that are meant to turn you into a better person. I can already tell you I don't like the lesson you've planned for me.

Perhaps not, but I can assure you that once this is all over, you will feel better for the experience.

Now why doesn't that thought give me comfort?

Libby finished her meal as quickly as possible. She couldn't handle sitting there any longer watching people she knew but who obviously no longer recognized her.

Now there was only one problem. She was be-

ginning a new job today at the last place she
wanted to be.

She didn't need to ask for directions when it
was time to pay her tab and leave for work. Not
when she had worked there for the past six years.
Not when it was the same school she herself had
gone to and always visualized her daughter at-
tending.

Libby parked her car in the preschool parking
lot and watched cars pull in and the drivers drop
off their pint-size passengers. Her eyes stung with
tears as she watched little girls and boys run into
the building.

"I can't do this," she whispered.

Of course you can.

Her hands tightened on the steering wheel as if
she wished to take flight.

*Go on, Libby. Go in and face your greatest
fear.*

Libby took several deep breaths to calm her
racing pulse. Then she climbed out of the car and
slowly headed for the entrance.

Chapter Four

"I'm so pleased you could come to us on such short notice, Libby. What with the holidays coming up and all." With her low voice, constant smile and warm manner, along with her silver hair pulled back in an intricate knot and her flowery dress billowing around her calves, Regina Parker looked like every child's dream of the perfect grandmother.

Libby couldn't remember a time in her life when she hadn't known Miss Parker. She had attended the preschool. She had even fallen so deeply under the older woman's spell that her only dream was to grow up and come back to work with her. One of Libby's happiest days was her first day teaching at the school. And how she'd loved those times when Tyler picked her up in the afternoon!

No memories now, Libby. You're here to make new ones.

Libby wanted nothing more than to scream at Matthias—demand he appear, even. Luckily, she knew better. He'd just remain invisible and she'd look like a fool.

"I've heard wonderful things about your school, Miss Parker," she said in a low voice.

"Please, call me Miss Regina. Everyone here does. Let me introduce you to your class. You'll learn that we're somewhat informal here. The children learn, but teaching is done with games and crafts."

"It sounds like a wonderful way for them to learn," Libby replied truthfully. "I've always believed children learn more if you make the classroom a fun place where they enjoy finding out about new things."

Miss Parker's face lit up. "I could tell when I read your resumé that you would be a perfect addition to our staff." She stood up, reaching for a cane she'd been forced to use since she broke her hip the previous spring. "Now let me introduce you to your class."

Libby could feel her smile freeze on her face as she likewise stood and followed the older woman out of the office.

Her breakfast churned alarmingly in her stomach as she walked. The scent of violets drifted in the air toward her. Libby remembered it well as Miss Regina's trademark.

She suddenly remembered the older woman contacting her after her baby's death. How many times had she called? How often had she urged Libby to talk to her, and all Libby could do was whisper that she couldn't talk and quietly hang up? After some time, there'd been no more calls. Now she wished she'd allowed her mentor to draw her out. Perhaps things would have been different for her.

But you didn't wish to talk to her, did you? You preferred to wallow all alone in your pain, as if you were the only one to have suffered so.

Libby flinched at the blunt words spoken in her mind. Her stomach clenched again when they approached the second-to-last door on the right.

From the first day she'd started teaching here, this had been her classroom. Always she had headed for this room eager to work with her students.

Miss Regina smiled and opened the door, stepping back so Libby could enter first. A heavily pregnant woman seated in a low chair was reading from a storybook. At the sound of visitors, she looked up and smiled.

Libby wanted to cry. She felt as if she was looking at her own self more than a year ago.

"All right, my babies, who's going to help the whale out of her chair this time?" the woman said cheerfully.

"Me!"

"Me!"

Within seconds, six small children were circling the woman and carefully helping her to her feet. She gave each one a thank-you hug before turning to Miss Regina and Libby.

"I gather you're Libby." She smiled, holding out her hand. "I'm Bonnie Summers. As you can tell—" She patted her round tummy "—the kids are useful in helping me get to my feet. I'm to the point where I'm more than happy to spend the remaining months wallowing in a comfortable chair with my feet propped up."

Libby had no idea how she could muster up a smile, but she did as she took Bonnie's hand. She felt as if she was looking at herself the day she had greeted her replacement.

"Yes, I can imagine it would be easier for you," she murmured. "When are you due?"

"In two months, but I feel as if I've been pregnant all my life." Bonnie chuckled. "Let me introduce you to my crew." She turned to the tiny faces looking up at them expectantly.

One face in the back of the group caught Libby's attention. The little girl had strawberry blond hair pulled back in a straggly ponytail, tied with a dark green ribbon that matched the ribbon trim in her green corduroy pinafore. A sprinkling of freckles dotted her cheeks and nose. Her mouth was made for laughter, except there was no laughter on her face or in her eyes. Instead, she looked at Libby with a touch of sorrow and something else that she couldn't read.

Libby smiled as Bonnie put names to the faces. Each child stood up when his or her name was called, and walked over to shake the new teacher's hand.

Blake, who swaggered over and gave a quick bow at the waist before taking her hand, was obviously the class show-off. His black hair and blue eyes along with a quick grin told Libby he would be a guaranteed lady-killer in ten years.

Candi was the class pinup girl. Her pink corduroy pants and pink-and-white print knit top were as immaculate as her white tennis shoes. Her blond hair was gathered up with pink barrettes that allowed the curls to cascade down her back. Libby doubted the little girl would let even a speck of dirt to touch her.

Troy was self-important, sure to grow up to be the next mover and shaker in the business world. Little Lisa was the bouncy cheerleader type, and Libby knew she would find the girl a wonderful helpmate in the class. Josh was obviously the one who loved to make trouble. The tear in his jeans bore witness to his latest brush with adventure.

Bonnie also pointed out Danny, Tisha, Kenny, Lisa and a few other children, but it was still the little girl in the back that Libby's attention kept wandering to. Since she didn't come forward, Libby finally walked over to her and crouched down.

"And who are you?" she asked in a soft voice.

The girl offered her a shy smile and whispered, "Becca."

"Becca," she repeated. She touched the girl's nose with her finger. "Becca with freckles."

Becca giggled. "Mrs. Robinson says they're angel kisses."

"And who's Mrs. Robinson?"

"She takes care of me, since I don't have a mommy or daddy," she said matter-of-factly. "They got lost."

"Becca is in foster care," Bonnie said softly, coming up to stand by Libby. "She was found wandering the streets, with no idea what happened to her parents or where she came from. When Miss Regina read about her in the newspaper, she called Mrs. Robinson and suggested Becca come here. She was hoping interaction with other children would help her cope with her loss."

Libby's heart clenched at the thought of a child left with strangers. She quickly stood up.

"Are you saying she isn't from around here? That she was virtually abandoned by her parents?" she whispered so Becca wouldn't hear.

Bonnie's lovely face showed concern for the

little girl. "It's a strange case. There were no car accidents in the area around the time she was found, and with her being so young, it hasn't been easy to find out much more than her name and that she's four. I'm afraid she doesn't interact with the children very well. It's as if she feels she doesn't need anyone else in her world."

A child without a mother being watched by a mother who'd lost her own child. Libby couldn't even imagine who hurt more here.

The morning passed quickly as Bonnie graciously stepped back so Libby would be the one dealing with the children.

They first made up a game to help Libby learn their names, and during rest time, Bonnie showed Libby lesson plans and the two women discussed what the class had been doing for the past few months. It didn't take Libby long to realize how much she had missed teaching.

"It's amazing how close your ideas are to Miss Regina's," Bonnie marveled as they shared lunch. "Most new teachers who have worked elsewhere don't approve of her methods and aren't afraid to say so."

"I can imagine they don't stay long, then, do they?" Libby smiled. "It was easy to discover that small children learn faster when they have fun while doing so. I don't know about you, but I swear I still have nightmares about my fourth-grade teacher, who ran her classroom like a military boot camp."

"You, too?" Bonnie laughed. "Mrs. Kittridge was like that when I was in fourth grade, and I couldn't imagine there could be another one of her."

Libby's smile froze for a second. She should have known that Bonnie, close to her own age, would have studied under the same teacher.

"Maybe it's a prerequisite for fourth-grade teachers," she said lightly.

"That's why I knew I wanted to teach preschoolers. Not to mention how much I enjoy all the playtime we have," Bonnie said with a mischievous twinkle in her eyes. "Although it hasn't been as easy to get up and down the past few months. I'm letting you do all that for the next few days. We won't even mention what happened to me the time I got down in the beanbag chair last week."

Libby chuckled at the mental picture of the pregnant young woman ensconced in an extremely soft chair that didn't readily release its occupants.

"How many kids did it take to get you out of it?"

"More like three teachers. I was told not to do it again." She laughed. "Have you started looking for a place to stay yet?"

Libby shook her head. "I haven't been here long enough. I know I can't put it off for too long. I guess I should start looking this weekend." In a sense, she felt reluctant to leave the motel. A part of her feared she would lose Matthias if she moved elsewhere.

Never fear, Libby. I will not leave you until it's time. I also told you that you would not be staying in a hotel for long.

You're such a comfort Matthias.

I try.

"If you don't need anything fancy, I know my aunt is looking for a tenant for the apartment over her garage. It's pretty roomy and set back on the property so you actually have privacy. She's a widow and does a lot of traveling, so she likes to know someone's around when she's gone."

"If it saves me from apartment hunting I'd be more than happy to look at it."

"I'll call Aunt Cyn and let her know you'll be by."

After that, Libby felt as if she was well on her way to making her first friend.

Libby was kept busy, which made the day go by fast for her.

She had forgotten how much fun it was to be with kids this age and also how much she could learn from them. But it was Becca her gaze turned to more and more often, and she couldn't help wondering about the little girl.

During storytime, Becca sat close to the front of the group arranged in a half circle, but she still managed to remain apart from the others. And on the playground, she preferred pieces of equipment she could use by herself.

How could parents just abandon a child like Becca? Libby wondered to herself.

There's always a reason, whether we understand it or not.

You're beginning to sound like Confucius.

Where do you think the man learned about true philosophy? There was no mistaking the arrogance in Matthias's tone.

By the end of the day, Libby was exhausted, but she felt more relaxed than she had in some time. If she had looked at herself in the mirror, she would have seen that her cheeks were flushed from her busy day and her smile came more readily.

She was busy straightening up the books when she noticed she wasn't alone in the room. Becca sat quietly in a chair, her hands in her lap and her coat lying on the table beside her. A Winnie the Pooh backpack leaned against her feet.

"Mrs. Robinson is late sometimes," Becca explained in her soft, whispery voice.

Libby walked over to the table and crouched

down on her heels so she was at eye level with the child.

"Do you like Mrs. Robinson, Becca?" she asked.

Becca's shoulders rose and fell in a shrug, as if she wasn't sure what to say. "She lets me help her make cookies," she replied. "And she has a cat. But King Tut is really old and he doesn't like to play. He smells funny, too."

Libby's lips curved. "So he doesn't like kids, huh?"

"He doesn't like anybody but Mrs. Robinson, and even she can't get him to smell nice," Becca confided. "I tried putting some of Mrs. Robinson's perfume on him once, but he got mad and scratched me. See?" She pulled back a sleeve and revealed a long, dark pink scratch along the inside of her arm.

"Cats aren't very fond of perfume," Libby said, feeling her facial muscles work overtime as she struggled not to laugh after hearing about the irate cat.

Becca looked past Libby. Libby turned to find a woman in her sixties enter the room.

"You must be Miss Libby. I'm Ada Robinson, Becca's foster mother." The woman smiled warmly. "I'm sorry I'm late. The Ladies Aid Society meeting ran longer than usual. Are you ready, Becca?"

The little girl nodded and stooped down to pick up her knapsack. She looked up at Libby.

"Goodbye, Miss Libby," she whispered, before following the woman out of the room.

Libby settled in the chair Becca had just vacated. For a moment, she felt very cold.

"I promised myself not to leave myself open for any more hurt," she whispered. It took several minutes before she could rouse herself to move. She had just finished straightening the books when Bonnie bustled in, walking in the modified duck waddle all pregnant women seem to have.

"Aunt Cyn will be more than happy to see you," she announced. "She said if you'd like to come by tonight she'll be home all evening." She held out a piece of paper with a name, address, phone number and directions.

"This is very nice of you," Libby murmured, studying the paper.

Bonnie waved off her comment. "You need a place to live and you may as well find a nice one. Besides, you don't want a motel to eat up all your money, do you?"

"No," Libby admitted, privately wondering just how much money she had. She still felt in the dark about a lot of things.

I would not worry if I were you. You have enough until you receive a paycheck.

"I'll call her. Thank you." She tucked the piece of paper in her skirt pocket.

"See you tomorrow." Bonnie picked up a patchwork-quilt bag. "Unless one day was too much for you," she joked.

Libby looked around the room, with its brightly colored posters on the walls, along with examples of the children's artwork. She wondered why she had fought for so long returning to school, when this was where she truly belonged.

"No, one day wasn't enough for me," she murmured.

The moment Libby got back to the motel, she pulled the paper out of her pocket and dialed the number.

"Cyn here!" a woman's husky voice answered.

Libby was taken aback by the robust, unorthodox greeting and couldn't think of anything to say for a moment. She could only sit there holding the receiver.

"If this is supposed to be an obscene phone call, I do wish you'd say something and make my day," the woman said.

"I'm sorry. I'm Libby Douglas. Your niece, Bonnie, told me to call you about the apartment," she said.

"Oh yes, the new teacher. What time would you like to come by?"

"Is seven all right?" Libby racked her brain to figure out if she knew Cyn or not. Considering the town wasn't all that large, she assumed she did. But nothing about the woman seemed familiar.

"Fine with me. Did Bonnie give you directions...? Good," she stated when Libby assured her she had. "I'll see you then." She hung up as abruptly as she'd answered the call.

Libby replaced the receiver in the cradle and wondered what she was going to do next.

"What would I do if I were in my own home?" she said in a louder voice, in hopes Matthias would hear her.

You never seemed to find anything constructive to do, as I recall.

Stung by his words, even if they only echoed in her head, she sat cross-legged in the middle of the bed. She had slipped off her shoes before climbing on the mattress and now she contemplated her black-stockinged toes. She knew she should go out to get some dinner, but she couldn't summon any enthusiasm for the idea.

She thought of all the times she'd been content to sit in the rocking chair in her room at home, just moving back and forth. She had sat there with Sara for hours, the few months she'd been allowed to hold her child in her arms. She would never forget the satisfaction of feeling the tiny body against hers as she nursed. Or the nights, especially the nights, when Tyler would sit up against the headboard, holding Libby against his chest while Libby either nursed Sara or just cuddled her.

If she closed her eyes, she could hear Tyler's voice softly rumbling in the dark as he predicted that Sara would say Daddy before she said Mommy. Or that he wouldn't allow her to date until she was at least thirty. Not to mention his musing that he should find himself a good shotgun for any boys who dared to sniff around his gorgeous daughter. No matter that Sara hadn't even started eating solid food yet or tried any word at all. Tyler had been convinced his daughter was the smartest, most beautiful kid in the world.

Libby's eyes snapped open and a tiny sob escaped her lips before she could stop herself. It wasn't long before the tears were flowing freely down her cheeks and she was rolling over to cry into her pillow.

She knew why she was crying. This was the first time she didn't have someone to comfort her in her sorrow.

Chapter Five

Libby looked at the address written on the paper, then up at the numbers painted on the side of the house near the front door. They matched.

Before she could ring the bell, the door opened. A woman wearing a flowing caftan stood in the light.

"You must be Libby. Come in, dear." She ushered Libby through the doorway.

The moment Libby stepped inside, she could smell the pungent aroma of burning incense and hear Asian music playing softly in the background. She turned to the woman.

Libby was positive Cyn's hair, piled high on her head in intricate curls, couldn't really be that outrageous shade of red. Her silk caftan was a green color somewhere between a bilious lime and kiwi. Libby decided it wouldn't have been so bad if it wasn't for the bright orange poppies bordering the hem. Large emeralds dotted Cyn's ears, throat and wrists, and when she walked, Libby couldn't miss the emerald-studded toe ring. Her energy level was that of a woman in her twenties, but the lines around her eyes and mouth and the experience in her gaze showed her age to be much closer to sixty.

"Hello, Libby, I'm Cyn," the woman said with a throaty laugh as she held out her hand. "Naturally, it's short for Cynthia, but I love to make my brother crazy by using the nickname. He's more than a little anal retentive at times." She narrowed her eyes, studying Libby. "Bonnie thought you might like the privacy the garage apartment offers. And she felt I'd like you. The thing I wonder is if you think you can handle being around someone like me."

Libby took on a reflective pose. "Does this mean you hold wild parties all the time and there're men coming and going at all hours?"

"Orgies are held monthly. You have a standing invitation. The bikers usually don't show up until spring." She waved her hand toward the living room. "Would you like a glass of wine?"

"That sounds wonderful."

"Have a seat and I'll bring a glass in for you."

Libby took in the furniture with a wary eye. Every piece was modular, in bright reds, blues and purples. The effect should have been jarring to the senses, but surprisingly, it wasn't. She was a little worried about the chair that looked more like a bowl, but even that turned out to be comfortable. She jumped a little when the music abruptly switched to the Rolling Stones.

"I guess you can already tell I'm the rebel in the family," Cyn announced, walking out of the kitchen carrying a large tray filled with two wineglasses, a bottle of wine, and crackers and cheese. "Bonnie said you're taking over for her. Good thing, too. I looked at her just the other day and I was positive the baby was ready to pop right out." She poured wine into the glasses and handed one to Libby.

Libby sipped the liquid and found it tart and refreshing.

"Do you have paperwork you'd like me to fill out?" she asked, reaching for a slice of cheese.

Cyn shook her head. "I dislike paperwork. Bonnie likes you and that's enough for me. I can imagine, though, you'll want to see the place before you decide on it." She stood up. "Bring your wine with you."

Libby hopped up to follow Cyn's energetic stride through a kitchen that looked as if it had stepped out of the 1950s, sparkling and new.

"Please don't worry that the apartment might be another facet of my personality," Cyn assured the younger woman as they crossed a large backyard to a three-car garage. "While I enjoy my oddities, I understand others might not. I don't believe in pushing my taste on others." She headed for a set of well-lit stairs that ran up the side of the garage. "The outside lights are on a sensor and come on at dusk."

Libby again quickened her pace to keep up with the older woman.

The small living room was furnished with a cream-and-blue-and-peach couch and an easy chair. A portable television was set on a small table. The tiny kitchen was meant for cooking for one, with every appliance in easy reach. Libby looked in the bedroom and found light wood furniture with a mauve-and-blue comforter on the bed.

All she would have to do to move in was pack her clothing and pick up groceries. "How much do you want for rent?"

Cyn quoted a price that was much lower than Libby expected.

Libby grinned. "If you want a tenant, you have one. I can move in tomorrow night."

Cyn smiled and held up her glass of wine. The two women touched glasses in a toast.

THE NEXT MORNING, Libby had no problem waking up on time. At first, when she opened her eyes, she hoped she would be back where she belonged. That perhaps even Tyler would be sprawled out beside her, his mouth slightly open as he emitted soft snores.

Then she would roll over and curl up against him, savoring the heat of his skin. She would lightly scratch her fingernails across his chest. She'd wait for that slow smile to cross his face. Then his hands would suddenly shoot out and grab her, tickling her, demanding she apologize for interrupting his sleep. Knowing she was ticklish, he would increase his efforts until she was screaming with laughter. Then the laughter would stop as his mouth covered hers and his hands slowed, the tickles turning into caresses as their play evolved into another type of play.

She moaned at the memory. Just as quickly, she recalled something else. She and Tyler hadn't made love since Sara died.

Libby sprang out of bed before the memories could completely swamp her. But even a cold shower couldn't shock her into accepting the alternate reality she was trying to deal with now.

"I am never making another wish," she vowed as she pulled on brown tights, then dressed in a cream-colored mock-turtleneck top and a brown corduroy jumper. While the jumper hung shapeless on the hanger, it gave life to her slender curves. "I will never blow out another birthday candle. I will never drop a coin in a wishing well. I will never break another wishbone. I will never look at another falling star!'' She picked up a pair of tortoiseshell studs and added a matching pendant. A touch of pumpkin-colored lipstick was last and she was ready to go.

The day passed quickly for Libby. It wasn't until rest time for the children that she thought again of Tyler. While Bonnie watched over the classroom, Libby made a quick run down to the office, and, luckily, found it empty. She looked for the telephone book and quickly turned to the *B*'s. She ran her finger down the listing until she found the one she wanted.

As she stared at Tyler's name and address in print, she could feel her heart turning over. The address was familiar; the telephone number was not.

Then another thought occurred to her. What if Tyler was married?

You do have a worry streak, don't you? If you are to work things out, would I have allowed him to be married?

''How would I know? He might be married if you thought I'd be better off with someone else or by myself,'' she muttered, closing the phone book and sneaking back to her classroom.

THE MOMENT HER WORKDAY was over, Libby went to the motel and packed her car with her belongings. She was glad it didn't take too long, since she wanted to do some grocery shopping next.

It still hurt seeing people she knew and who obviously didn't know her as she roamed the grocery store, picking up what she needed.

When she exited the store, she could feel her face stretching into a smile.

Then she glanced in the direction of a barbecue restaurant at one end of the shopping center. It wasn't the restaurant as much as the couple walking toward it that caught her attention.

Her stomach tightened into painful knots.

Her throat dried up.

Her skin burned.

She wanted to kill.

It wasn't so much seeing Tyler Barnes, who was supposed to be her husband. It was seeing the woman with him that poured acid into her system.

Then it happened.

As if aware of her scrutiny, he turned his head and glanced over his shoulder. He was looking straight at her! Their gazes locked and held for a moment before the woman next to him said something to catch his attention.

Libby's fingers tightened on the cart's handle, so she wouldn't fall to the ground.

Her loving, wonderful husband was walking with the woman who had been Libby's high-school rival. He was with a woman she practically hated with a vengeance. A woman who'd tried every trick in the book to snag Tyler. Libby had made sure Renee never got her hooks into him.

Or at least, she'd thought she had....

"Take off your coat, Renee. I want to see if you still have chubby thighs," she muttered with feminine malice.

Chapter Six

"I cannot believe he is actually dating Renee Carter," Libby muttered darkly. She unlocked her car door and tossed her purse onto the passenger seat. With anger still boiling deep inside her, she began throwing packages into the back. They bounced onto the seat as if they were eager to get away from her. "How could he forget what she's like? She was with every boy in the senior class when she was a freshman!" Renee had a notorious reputation. She had even said she worked hard to get that reputation—and was more than happy to flaunt it no matter who she hurt in the process.

Libby continued raining curses on Tyler and Renee as she drove to Cyn's.

And here I thought you'd be happy to have a chance to see your Tyler.

"Happy to see him with *her?*" Libby asked incredulously. "I don't think so, Matthias. That wasn't fair at all. I'm sent into an alternate world where my husband is cozying up with the woman most likely to do just about anything to make a man happy. Actually, she has done just about anything to make a man happy.''

Likely to make happy? In what way?

"I'm talking about her intimately knowing every guy in school before the year was out." She parked the car in front of the garage. "Damn her bleached blond head." She climbed out of the car and went back to the trunk.

"There you are, darling!" Cyn sang out, walking out the back door. This time she was attired in a peacock blue caftan and gold sandals. Scarlet nails peeked out from the thin straps of her shoes. "Would you like some help?"

"No, thank you. I don't have a lot."

"Well, once you finish, come on over. I have a lovely dinner waiting for us. Just walk in." In a flurry of peacock silk she went back inside.

With Libby's temper still simmering, it didn't take her long to unload the car and take everything upstairs. After stowing the perishables in the refrigerator, she changed her clothes and headed back downstairs to Cyn's.

When she entered the kitchen, a rich, mouthwatering scent tickled her nostrils. Cyn stood at the stove ladling stew into two bowls.

"A secret recipe, and I never tell anyone what I put in it," she informed Libby after gesturing for her to sit. She set the bowls on the table along with a basket of warm sourdough rolls.

It took only one spoonful for Libby to know it was one of the best stews she'd ever tasted. "As long as you don't tell me there's yak or crocodile in this, I don't care," she told her in between spoonfuls. "This is fantastic."

"So you won't mind if it's rattlesnake?"

Libby's head snapped upward and she probably would have screamed if she hadn't seen the crafty look in the older woman's eyes.

"Only if you left the rattles out. They're always so nice and chewy."

Cyn smiled. "Now, tell me what you think of our town so far," she urged.

A part of Libby wanted to confide in Cyn about her true niche in the town, but she feared Cyn wouldn't believe her and might think she wasn't all there. Or even worse, she would believe her story and insist on trying some crazy hocus-pocus to get her back to her own reality.

It is never wise to bring others in, Libby. Cyn would understand, but she can't help you. Only you yourself can help you.

Libby postponed her reply by picking up a piece of bread and spreading butter on the warm surface.

"Everyone I've met seems very nice," she said

finally, opting for an answer she hoped a truly new person in town would give.

"I guess you haven't had a chance to meet any men," Cyn said. "And don't tell me you left someone behind because I can't imagine any man in his right mind letting you go."

Libby's smile was wistful. Tyler hadn't let her go; it was she who had let him go. "No, no one. That's why I'm here."

"Then we'll have to see about you meeting some nice young men. Bonnie knows about every event that goes on in this town. Actually, she knows what's happening in the whole county. She and her husband used to go dancing every weekend until a couple months ago. They still go out sometimes, but she says it's too difficult to dance now. I swear their baby will come out dancing."

"I would think you're no slouch in the social department," Libby said with a sly smile as she sipped the wine Cyn had served with the stew.

The older woman preened under the sincere praise. "I must admit that Harold Lutz thinks I'm pretty hot." She patted the intricate curls piled high on her head. Two onyx chopsticks with tiny pearls dangling from the ends had been plunged among the bright red curls. "We've known each other since grade school and I'm sad to say that takes a little of the mystery out of it. Not to mention he's someone who prefers to stick close to home, while I'm usually adding another stamp to my passport.''

Libby thought of Tyler. ''But sometimes isn't it nice to know someone who has no secrets from you?'' she asked.

Cyn clicked her tongue. ''Darling, everyone deserves a few secrets. It gives the relationship some spice. If you know someone as well as you know yourself, there are no surprises for you. No excitement to rev up the senses. And believe me, an old lady like me enjoys those surprises just as much as a young woman like you does. You need a young man who will give you all the spice and surprises.''

Libby decided it wouldn't hurt to test the waters.

''I haven't heard about too many men, but one name that's come up is Tyler Barnes,'' she mentioned as casually as she could.

Cyn bestowed on her a smile filled with cunning pride. ''My, my, Libby, you are a daring one. That Tyler is more than hunk material. He's every woman's dream. Too bad Renee Carter has him tied up with a big red bow. People have been taking bets as to when they'll set a wedding date.''

Dismay settled in Libby's stomach like a lump of lead.

Cyn shook her head. ''Renee tried to hook him

back in high school, but he's a wily one. She left in a huff and married a computer programmer who moved her to Kansas City. She got a divorce a few years ago and moved back here. Her public reason was to be close to her parents, but we all know she's still hoping to snare Tyler.''

See what happens when you want Tyler out of your life? He gets caught up with wild women.

Libby instantly thought of a few choice responses to Matthias's less-than-gentle reminder.

Ah, ah, ah, a lady doesn't use words like that.

At this moment, you non corporeal being, I'm not a lady!

She was startled to notice Cyn watching her with an intensity that was unsettling.

''You have such an interesting aura,'' Cyn murmured. ''I studied auras under a wonderful psychic who lives outside of London. She could look at people and immediately know a lot about them just by studying their energy field.''

''Really?'' Libby said with a brightness that felt incredibly forced.

Cyn nodded, still studying Libby. ''I have a knack in seeing auras. Yours is intriguing,'' she murmured. ''It's filled with the many changes in your life. And you will have even more changes in the near future.'' She stared at Libby, but her gaze appeared to be looking at something not visible to the naked eye.

Libby shifted uncomfortably under the woman's close scrutiny.

"You're not going to tell me I have food on my sweater, are you?" she asked in light voice in hopes of changing the mystical mood hanging over them.

Cyn blinked several times. It was as if she'd just come out of a trance.

"You're here to make choices, aren't you?" she said in a quiet voice. "Choices that will affect the rest of your life."

The room may have been warm, but Libby could swear she felt a chill clear through to her bones.

"Isn't a choice always involved when one moves to a new locale?"

Cyn shook her head. "Not the choice you're here to make." Concern etched her features. "Oh, Libby, what have you gotten yourself into?"

"The only thing I've gotten myself into is moving to a new town and taking a new job," she replied, lying without a qualm.

She remained as calm as she could under Cyn's analytical gaze. The older woman still looked skeptical, but didn't contradict her. Libby knew she'd have to watch her step around Cyn.

"Tell me how your second day with the little darlings went. Have they driven you into a strait jacket yet?" Cyn asked as she picked up her glass of wine. "Some of the stories Bonnie told me were almost scary. Perhaps that's why I never had children. They can be so unpredictable at times."

Libby told Cyn about one of Josh the trouble-maker's escapades. That afternoon, he had flushed Candi's doll down a toilet—a caper that nearly caused a flood in the bathroom and a flood of tears from Candi.

"At that age, unpredictable is just a part of their charm," Libby said. "But there's one little girl who, sadly, is having problems with the class." She recalled how Becca stayed to herself most of the day unless Libby and Bonnie urged her to join the others. "Her name is Becca. No one is sure whether her parents just abandoned her or what. And she doesn't know enough about her family to give the authorities any help in finding them. So she's presently in foster care."

Cyn nodded. "Bonnie told me about her. Poor little thing, to just be left like that. Bonnie said the authorities are still trying to look for her family. If only she could tell them something."

"The thing is, you just look at her and you want to gather her into your arms. You want to promise nothing bad will ever happen to her," Libby murmured.

Cyn reached across the table and covered her hand with her own. "Then that's just what you do, darlin'. You hold on to her."

IT WAS LATE before Libby collapsed into bed. Still, she had trouble sleeping. Too many memories of Tyler kept her from closing her eyes.

The worst memory for her was the image of Tyler looking back at her tonight in the parking lot. No, not looking at her, she sadly corrected herself. He'd looked *through* her because he had no idea who she was.

How could he not remember her? She could recall all the memories they'd made together. Why couldn't he?

She was the one who'd shared her cream-filled cupcakes with him. She'd loaned him her math homework so he could pass that class in eighth grade. She'd brought him burgers and shakes when he was stuck at home with the chicken pox.

But he was the one who'd cried after they'd made love for the first time, because he hadn't realized how magical their union would be.

"What are you regretting now?"

Libby sat up in bed and squinted through the darkness. It took a moment for her eyes to become accustomed to the lack of light. By then she could see a faint figure seated in the chair by the window.

"It's not fair that he's with someone else."

Matthias smiled. "Who said life is fair?"

Libby thrust her fingers through her hair. "By rights, I should be telling myself this is a bad dream. That all I have to do is wake up and I'll discover everything is back to the way it was."

"My dear, you want a perfect life and there is no such thing. You have to learn that life goes on no matter what. Self-pity can last only so long, Libby," he continued in a softer voice. "It was time for you to move on with your life. Don't worry, you'll know when you've done just that." He disappeared as abruptly as he'd appeared.

She flopped back on her pillows, contemplating his words. "I still say it's unfair."

"Why can't you just stay here?" Renee pouted as Tyler left her house, tucking his shirt back in his jeans.

"I have an early day tomorrow," he said as he strode to his truck. "We're starting on that new job."

"But, honey," Renee practically whined, rushing after him. She threw her arms around him and pressed her body against his. "I'll even make you breakfast," she cooed.

Tyler grinned and pressed a hard kiss against her lips. "You wicked woman, you. Are we talking Belgian waffles and maple syrup?"

She stepped back, a pout on her face. "Well, no." Everyone knew Renee didn't cook. It was considered practical to keep her out of the kitchen at all costs. "But what's so wrong with staying the night? Afraid of your reputation?"

"You got it." He kissed her again to halt further pouting. "I'll pick you up at seven Friday night."

"Maybe I won't be here," she said loftily, tossing her head.

Tyler knew better. Renee would act as if she couldn't care less, but she'd be there waiting for him.

"See you then." He climbed in his truck. "Now get inside before you freeze into a beautiful Popsicle."

Tyler glanced in his rearview mirror as he drove off. Renee still stood in the yard, her robe wrapped tightly around her body.

Renee Carter had been prom queen and homecoming queen their junior and senior year in high school. And Tyler had been only one of many who'd wanted to be king to her queen. Not to mention get in her pants. Many boys were grief stricken when she'd left town after graduation and settled in a nearby town to go to college. It was even worse when word came back that she'd married.

When she got a divorce four years ago and returned to town, Tyler was one of the first to invite her out. Since then they'd seen each other at least once a week.

Tyler knew a lot of people figured they'd get married sooner or later. And maybe they would. But hell, he wasn't even thirty yet. He had his whole life ahead of him. He wasn't going to be pushed into anything he wasn't ready for. Not to mention he kind of hoped Renee would start taking some cooking classes.

He suddenly remembered his comment about Belgian waffles. Why had he asked her that? He couldn't remember if he'd ever had anything other than plain old waffles.

When he reached his house, he parked his truck in the driveway and walked into the house. He stopped in the kitchen long enough to snag a beer from the refrigerator before heading for the living room. The house was chilly, so he kept his jacket on as he drank his beer.

He felt unsettled, almost out of sorts. He wasn't sure why, not after the night he'd just had—dinner out with Renee, then back to her place. Except a face kept intruding.

Because it had been dark and the parking lot wasn't well lit, he hadn't been able to make out the woman's features very well, but he felt as if he'd seen her before. Light-colored hair, medium height, body looking bulky because of the heavy coat she wore. Trim ankles...Every once in a while, his thoughts would occasionally travel back to her. Why?

He wished he knew.

It wouldn't take long to find out who she was. That was the nice thing about small towns— someone new always attracted attention. Ironically, Tyler hadn't even thought about whether she might be married or not. In his heart he couldn't consider that problem.

Chapter Seven

Libby literally flew down the stairs to the garage door. She couldn't believe she'd slept right through her alarm.

"Have a good day!" Cyn sang out from her backyard, where she was busy putting out plastic sheets and extra soil to protect her flowers during the harsh winter.

Libby arrived at school before Bonnie and took a turn around the classroom to make sure everything was in order. She straightened up a stack of books and under the shelves found a couple of crayons that she dropped in one of the crayon buckets.

When she turned back around, she found Miss Regina standing in the doorway.

"I came by to tell you that Bonnie won't be in today. She has a doctor's appointment this morning and talked about coming in after she was finished. I told her you seemed to be able to handle the children just fine on your own."

"I hope everything is all right," Libby said with concern. Recollection of her own uncomplicated pregnancy with Sara flitted through her brain.

Miss Regina placed her hand on her arm for reassurance. "I think she's just anxious to have her baby. She said she's tired of not seeing her feet. By the way, Bonnie has an aide come in some days, which helps when you have the children doing an art project."

Libby grinned. "Don't worry, I'll keep the whips and handcuffs nearby in case they threaten to revolt."

"Wow! We saw a car crash into another car, and I think one guy's head rolled on the street!" Josh loudly announced as he bounced into the room. He hopped over to the cubicles where the children kept their lunch boxes and coats and stashed his Batman lunch box in one that was marked with his name. He pulled off his coat and threw it in after his lunch box. "It was really cool. I even saw blood on the road!"

"I'd say someone got into the sugary cereal today," Miss Regina murmured as she left the room. "Oh my, he's going to be a handful this morning."

"You're more than welcome to stay!" Libby called after her.

"Don't worry, dear. I have confidence in you."

With the wave of children streaming in the door, Libby's workday had begun.

SO SHE'S A BLONDE.

Tyler stood at attention with a drill in his hand as he stared across the busy construction site to the crowded playground.

His attention was mainly centered on the young woman supervising a game of dodgeball. She appeared to be having as much fun as the kids were.

Since she was bundled up against the cold, her figure was hidden from him, but what he could see he liked.

"Some boss you are if you can't keep your mind on the work," a grizzled man in coveralls told him around the cigar he was chomping on. He looked in the same direction as Tyler. "No wonder. She's a honey, all right."

Another man joined them. "She must be the teacher who's replacing Bonnie."

"So she's single?"

"Yep."

"I sure wouldn't mind taking her out dancing."

"Yeah, I bet she could teach me a few things."

Tyler was silent during the exchange. He couldn't stop watching her. He wasn't sure why, but he could swear he was feeling stirrings of what he could only think of as jealousy. And he didn't even know the woman's name! Yet he felt as if he *should* know it.

She wasn't close by, but he could swear he could smell the vanilla fragrance of her perfume. He knew all about the way her smile tilted up one side of her lips. He knew she'd have an honest-to-God giggle when she was truly happy. And could he smell waffles and maple syrup?

"Good morning, gentlemen. I'm glad to see you have nothing better to do than stand around wishing you were over there playing on the swings and teeter-totters," a male voice barked.

They practically sprang to attention. Fred Chambers had been a drill sergeant in the Marine Corps until he retired and started up a construction company in his hometown. Just because he owned the company didn't mean he stayed in an office. He was happier working on-site with his men while his wife ran the office. All his years in the marines had honed his command skills to a fine point. Along with his voice.

Fred glared at Tyler. "What about you, Barnes? Since you're standing around acting like some floppy dog, I gather you have your section done."

"I'm just about there, Boss," he said, almost saluting. Past episodes warned him it wouldn't be a good idea, even as a joke. "Sorry. I just wanted to look at something that brightens up the day."

Fred glanced at the playground. "If you know what's good for you, you won't be looking at other women. I've heard Renee can be pretty ruthless if she thinks someone's poaching on her property. That little girl over there could end up getting hurt."

Tyler's features hardened at his words. "Considering I'm *no one's* property, I'd say no one needs to worry about taking the good suit out of the closet anytime soon."

Fred chuckled and shook his head. "Well, son, that's what they all say. But they still get hooked and reeled in before they know what's going on."

ALL DURING THE TIME she was on the playground, Libby could feel Tyler's gaze fastened on her. She didn't know why he watched her so intently when he didn't even know her. His staring made a familiar warm feeling well up inside her.

Libby enjoyed rest time, when the children would lie down on special mats with blankets they'd brought from home for their naps. In the old days, she had usually read during this period, and it was easy to fall back into the habit. Except now she would occasionally lift her head and look over at one little girl curled up under a tattered yellow blanket. Becca's eyes were open and she was watching Libby.

Libby got up and walked over to her. She crouched down and touched Becca's shoulder.

"Shouldn't you be resting?" she whispered. "The dodgeball game seems to have worn everyone else out."

"I'm not tired. Besides, I like looking at you," Becca whispered back.

Libby smiled. "Thank you."

"I want to look like you when I grow up," she told her in her whispery voice.

"Maybe you will. When I was your age my hair was the same color yours is now." She lightly touched a stray strand. "And I had lots of freckles. But I wasn't like you. I hated them."

"You forgot. They're not freckles, they're angel kisses," Becca whispered. "They mean angels watch over us."

"I wish I'd known that when I was your age. I might not have tried so hard to get rid of them." She smoothed back the little girl's hair.

For a moment, she thought of her baby, who had had red-gold hair at birth. If Sara had lived, she probably would have looked like Becca when she grew to Becca's age. Is that what drew her to the little girl? Or the fact that she had no parents, just as Libby no longer had a child?

Or a husband, she wryly reminded herself.

Ah, but you didn't want your husband, remember?

Libby pasted a smile on her lips, patted Becca's shoulder and straightened up.

I didn't exactly ask for you to interfere in my life.

Oh yes, you did.

Says you. I'm beginning to think you're not any type of angel. You were just sent to make my life hell.

Entities aren't angels. Nor are we allowed to participate in any evil rituals.

Libby picked up her book and sat down to read. She glanced at the clock. Rest time had another ten minutes to go.

Tell you what, Matthias, why don't you go bother Cyn? I'm sure she'd love your company.

I'm sorry, Libby, I'm all yours.

She felt a sigh rippling through her body.

Until I say I was wrong? Fine. I was wrong. I want my old life back. I've said it before and I'm saying it again. Or do I have to take a blood oath?

You need to understand yourself more, Libby. You need to see what's truly important to you. You took the first step when you came into this classroom instead of running away.

Libby wasn't sure how she knew, but she

sensed Matthias's departure, which was as abrupt as always.

You'd think he'd at least say goodbye.

LIBBY WAS GLAD she was able to match parents' faces with each child and by now could even greet most of them by name.

"I have to admire your courage taking on all these kids," Marian, Josh's mother, told her. "Josh, leave the hamster alone! I can't imagine they all have Josh's energy, thank God, but they still have to be a handful. Josh, there is no reason to tease the rabbit!"

Libby stood there, openly amazed by Marian's calm handling of her son, who hadn't stopped running around since his mother had arrived.

"You're the one who deserves a medal. I understand you have more at home."

Marian, a spritely brunette, laughed. "We have eight more at home."

Libby's eyes widened. "Nine children?"

"When my husband said he wanted a large family I had no idea he meant that large. But I quickly discovered pregnancy agreed with me. I never had morning sickness with any of them."

"The way you look I'd say that handling your kids is better than aerobics," Libby said.

"Only where the boys are concerned." Marian reached out and grabbed Josh's hand, pulling him up short when he ran past them. "Stand still for five seconds," she ordered. "No wonder poor Miss Libby looks frazzled, if she's had to run after you all day." Her gaze was caught by Becca, who was sitting across the room. "Has there been any word on finding her family yet?" she asked in a low voice.

Libby shook her head. "They just don't have enough to go on. I understand notice has been sent out to all law agencies in Indiana and the surrounding states, but so far no word."

Marian *tsked* as she shook her head. "Such a pretty little thing to be put into the system. Poor baby. It must be difficult for her, since she appears to be so shy."

"I was that way when I was her age." Libby smiled. "Then a little boy pulled me out of my shy state."

"Boys will do that, won't they? And they're always so darn cute then, too." Marian chuckled. "Well, we're off. I'm glad to know Josh isn't being a total terror. Maybe it's because he adores you."

Libby was amused to know a boy who could turn a woman's hair gray overnight adored her.

"I hate to think what he'd do if he couldn't stand me," she said lightly.

Marian shuddered. "I don't think you want to

know. Come on, monster boy." She pulled on Josh's hand.

"Bye, Miss Libby!" he shouted as he instantly took the lead and pulled his mother out of the room.

"Miss Libby?"

Libby turned around at the whispered sound of her name. Becca stood nearby, looking uncertain.

"Mrs. Robinson is outside in her car," the little girl murmured. "Her arthritis is acting up so she doesn't want to get out of the car if she doesn't have to. Can I go?"

Miss Regina's rules were strictly enforced. Children could not leave the classroom unless a parent or authorized adult came to pick them up.

"I'll tell you what. I'll go out with you," Libby offered, holding out her hand. "Let's get your coat on, shall we?"

As she crouched down and buttoned up Becca's coat, she noticed that the sleeves were too short for her thin arms and were tight in the shoulders. The garment also looked a little threadbare.

For a moment she wanted to pull the little girl into her arms for a hug, but she sensed Becca would recoil from any type of sympathy.

"You must be growing like a weed," she commented lightly, smoothing down the collar. She straightened up and took Becca's hand. "Now let's get out there before Mrs. Robinson thinks

Josh flushed you down the commode," she whispered. She was gratified to hear a hint of a giggle in return.

They walked outside and along the walkway to the parking lot, where a gray sedan waited. Smoke billowed out of the tailpipe to battle with the cold air.

Mrs. Robinson smiled and waved at Libby. She opened the window. "I'm sorry you had to come out here with Becca," she said. "This cold weather just doesn't treat these old bones kindly."

"No problem, Mrs. Robinson," Libby assured her, opening the passenger door and helping Becca onto the seat. "I hope you're taking it easy."

"Oh, I am." The older woman beamed at Becca. "My little one has been a big help."

"I'll see you tomorrow, Becca," Libby said as she stood back.

She watched them drive away before turning back to the school building. She smiled and waved when Becca swung her arm over her shoulder and waved at her.

"I gather Ada's arthritis is acting up again," Miss Regina commented when Libby entered the building.

Libby nodded.

The older woman sighed. "It's a shame that little girl is having to live with someone more the age of a grandmother than a mother. At the same time I guess we should consider her lucky to be with someone who's so good with children. And Ada loves to bake, which always endears her to any child's heart. And she does what she can with her charges.'' Miss Regina studied Libby. ''You're a wonder with the children. I don't think I want you to marry and have children too soon.''

''I wouldn't worry about that,'' Libby said softly. ''It appears there's too much for me to do first.''

Chapter Eight

Libby turned the key in the ignition. All that could be heard was a faint click, then nothing.

"Dammit!" she muttered, pounding the steering wheel with her gloved fist. She jumped when she heard a tapping on the window.

Then her heart leaped when she looked up to see Tyler standing by her car door. She rolled down the window.

"I hate to tell you this, but it sounds as if you have a dead battery," he said with the easy grin that never failed to melt her insides. "Do you have any jumper cables? I can give you a jump start then."

"I don't think so," she said hesitantly, trying to remember what was in her trunk.

"Don't worry, I have some." He loped off toward a dark blue 4x4 pickup truck. A moment later he'd driven it toward her, so the hood faced the front of her car. He popped his hood, then gestured for her to do the same. Within minutes, he had the cables connected. Luckily, it didn't take long for her car to start up.

"Let's give it a minute just to be sure," he advised. He braced his crossed arms on the window. "I'm Tyler Barnes." He cocked an eyebrow, waiting for her to tell him her name.

"Libby Douglas," she murmured. She wasn't sure what to think of his bold gaze. She could already see this wasn't the Tyler she knew!

I told you things have changed.

"I sure hope that's *Miss* Libby Douglas?" He leaned a little closer.

The masculine aroma of male skin with a hint of sweat and soap assailed her senses as he invaded her space. Libby felt that if she hadn't been wearing a heavy coat he surely would have seen through her clothes! She wasn't sure she liked him acting this way.

"You're new in town," he said.

"I'm replacing Bonnie Summers," she explained.

"So you taught rug rats before you came here?"

Libby nodded. "I taught in Webster Falls, but I wanted a change. This position came up at the right time."

"Then it looks like we're the ones who are lucky," he said with a rakish grin. "So tell me,

Libby Douglas. What are you doing Friday night?''

This wasn't the Tyler she knew! At least he would have waited a little longer before asking her out. She remembered Tyler acting bold, but nothing like this!

"Relaxing and looking forward to the weekend, when I can finish my unpacking and get settled in.''

"I'm real good at unloading boxes.'' His grin was almost arrogant.

"I'm sure you are, but I don't have anything heavy to worry about. But thank you for the offer.''

"Just being neighborly.'' His grin widened. "After all, we'll be neighbors. I'm working on the new school building.'' He crooked his thumb over his shoulder in the direction of the construction site.

"Then all I ask is that you watch the language when the children are outside. There's no sense in teaching them new words too soon.'' She kept a smile on her lips that was polite but dismissive. She remembered Tyler used to call it her teacher's smile. "It was nice meeting you, Mr. Barnes. Thank you for helping me with my car.'' She pushed the gear stick into reverse and backed up.

Tyler stood there watching her drive off. "Sorry, honey, but all you've done is prime the fire," he murmured, still watching when the small car turned the corner. "You're not going to get away that easy."

"Tyler Barnes, are you trying to charm one of my teachers into going out with you?" There was no missing Miss Regina's imperious tone.

He turned around to face the teacher, who could intimidate a majority of her former students. Brash as he was, even he would never try to fool her.

"Yes, I am, Miss Regina." He knew it was best to be no less than honest with this woman. "I can't help it when I see a pretty woman."

She smiled. "I'm glad to see you didn't try to lie to me, Tyler. I'm going to make a suggestion and I hope you take it. Leave Libby alone. She hasn't lived here long enough to know what a rake you are."

"Now, Miss Regina, how could you call me that?" He pressed his palms against his chest in mock sorrow. "I'm always the model gentleman, thanks to your teaching."

She arched an eyebrow. "I am very serious, Tyler. Libby isn't your kind of woman. Although I'd hazard a guess she'd be better for you than your usual choice of companions."

If any other woman had said that to him, his hackles would have immediately risen and he would have offered a quick retort. But this was

Miss Regina, who had literally shaped his first years of life. No other woman in town commanded the respect Regina Parker did. And not just because the Parkers had been one of the town's founding families. She was the epitome of a lady and instilled gracious manners in her students.

"Renee Carter was one of your students here, too," he reminded her.

Miss Regina's lips pursed as if she had eaten a lemon. "Yes, and if I recall correctly, she wasn't one of my stellar students."

Renee had often been caught kissing the boys behind the playhouse.

Tyler knew when to quit. "Do you need any help getting to your car, Miss Regina?"

She looked down her nose at him. "Young man, the day I cannot make it to my own car is the day I'm carried out in a casket to Willow Hills Memorial Park. Now, I suggest you run along and do whatever you boys do on a night like this and let me lock up the school."

He did the only thing he could after the regal dismissal. He left.

LIBBY COULDN'T STOP thinking about Tyler during her drive to her apartment.

"All right, Matthias," she said out loud. "It's

time for you to explain why Tyler is acting that way.''

He's never had you in his life. He wasn't exactly a troublemaker during his school days, but he was known for finding all the wild parties and having fun all weekend.

''Well, there's fun, then there's fun. Right now he thinks he's God's gift to women, and with an attitude like that I wouldn't look twice at him.'' Her face crumpled. ''I want my old Tyler back! This Tyler didn't look at me as if I was a woman, a person. He looked at me as if he was wondering how long it would take him to get me into bed!''

That's Tyler, all right.

Libby wrinkled her nose in distaste. ''That is not Tyler! The man I just spoke to was not the man I fell in love with.''

Then why don't you show him just how lucky he would be to have you in his life? At the same time, you might discover how lucky you are to have him in yours.

''Your idea of lessons is extremely distressing,'' she answered, then wished she hadn't used that descriptive word the moment she drove down the driveway and parked in the garage.

The first thing she noticed was a vehicle parked near the back door. It was a blue Explorer. That might not have meant anything to her if she hadn't also seen the tan plush stuffed dog sprawled across the back seat.

She didn't have to peek inside the vehicle to know she'd find a floral eyeglass case lying on the passenger seat and a travel mug in the mug holder. She knew the driver hated leaving the house without coffee. Even if it was for a short drive across town.

Libby walked slowly across the yard and stopped by the utility vehicle. Her fingers brushed against the cold metal. She sought comfort where none was forthcoming.

"Libby, is that you?" Cyn sang out. She pushed open the back door and peered out. "Come in, dear. I want you to meet a good friend of mine."

With her head held high and her back straight, Libby mounted the steps and walked inside. Just as she expected, a woman in her late fifties sat at the table with a teacup in front of her.

"Marie, this is Libby Douglas. She's the teacher who's replacing Bonnie. Libby, this is Marie Bennett, a very close and dear friend of mine."

"Hello, Libby." Marie smiled warmly. "I've been hearing very good things about you from Cyn. Would you like to sit down and have some tea with us? On a day like today, it's guaranteed to warm your bones."

"Thank you." Libby fervently prayed her smile wasn't slipping as she politely greeted the woman she had always known as Mother. Now Marie didn't even know her. "It is very cold out there."

"I guess it's too soon to ask you what you think of Willow Hills." Marie picked up the teapot and poured tea into another cup. She handed it to Libby. "Cyn said you've only been here for a few days."

Libby smiled her thanks as she accepted the cup. She sipped the tea, allowing the liquid to warm her.

"I'm afraid I haven't seen much other than the motel I first stayed in, the school and then here," she admitted, taking a cookie off the plate set next to the teapot. She bit into it, finding the familiar taste of oatmeal, chocolate chips and a hint of cinnamon. Her mother had made these cookies—something else that saddened her. "These are very good."

"I'd love to say I baked them, but I'm not a very good baker. Marie brought these over along with some other goodies." Cyn's brilliant fuchsia tunic and top were accented with purple and turquoise jewelry.

"It's better to bring them over here than eat them myself," Marie said.

Libby took another cookie. "After running after kids all day, I can use the energy.'' She was prepared to sit there and just enjoy the company even if the older woman didn't realize the importance of this meeting.

When was the last time she'd spent any time with her mother? she wondered. Time the way they used to. Her memory shifted back to the last time they had gone out to lunch and just sat and talked. Or gone shopping. Or even gone to the park and enjoyed a sunny afternoon.

Sorrow filled her as she realized it had to have been before Sara's death. Afterward, Libby had shut herself away from the world so she could grieve. And in the process, she had shut everyone away from her.

"So you bring all these goodies over to Cyn," she said, this time choosing a buttery cookie dusted with colored sugar. How many times had she come home from school as a child and found these cookies lying on a plate?

Marie leaned over as if to impart a secret. "Cyn's very susceptible to my fudge brownies."

"It's because I don't bake," Cyn confessed. "Any cake I try baking either falls or turns out hard as a rock."

"At last year's Ladies' League picnic we used her cookies for Frisbees," Marie added.

"At least I never have to contribute to bake

sales. All they ever want is my money paying for the goodies the others bring.''

Libby burst out laughing. As she did, she realized this was one of the very few times she had laughed in the past several months. And it felt good.

"Now tell us about your day," Cyn suggested. "Did Josh try to flush anything else down the commode?" She quickly filled Marie in on the other Josh episode.

"No, thank goodness. He was actually somewhat well behaved today." Libby poured herself more tea, finding the orange spice brew soothing. "I think he's hoping to throw me off guard before he does something entirely wild."

Cyn nodded. "All the boys in that family are like that."

Marie chuckled. "I have all boys and they used to act just as bad. Thank God they're adults now and out of the house, though I don't think they'll ever grow up."

"No daughters?" Libby whispered. She understood why she didn't exist in Marie's life, but what about Vicky?

Marie's smile was tinged with regret. "No, I'm afraid not. I'd hoped for one or two girls to balance out the household, but I was never that lucky."

Libby didn't stop to think when she reached

across the table and covered Marie's hand with her own. "You should have had daughters to pass your baking skills on to."

Marie turned her hand over to gently squeeze Libby's. "Thank you, dear. But you learn to be happy with what you have because all children always seem to provide you with a special joy."

"Or a lot of headaches," Cyn murmured with a sly smile.

"This from the woman with four husbands."

Libby's mouth dropped open. *"Four?"*

Cyn shrugged. "What can I say? None of them could keep up with me."

Libby laughed as Cyn made wry comments about each of her ex-husbands.

"I probably would have remarried Henry if he hadn't gotten himself indicted for insider trading." She shook her head, *tsking* softly under her breath. "The man just loved playing the market, but he had a bad habit of not playing fair."

Libby found herself alternately laughing and wheezing as the two women went on to amiably bicker about which of them had been the more popular back in high school.

Marie was the first one to look up at the clock on the wall.

"I'd best get home to start dinner," she said, rising to her feet. "Nathan will be home before I know it."

Libby felt pain at the mention of her father—someone else she hadn't spent time with for many months. She wondered if he still had heart trouble. Was he taking his prescribed walks and his medication? Did he stay away from his favorite foods, which only worsened his condition? She hated that she couldn't ask.

"It was very nice meeting you, Libby," Marie said, as she put on her coat and buttoned it up. "When you're ready to meet some nice young men I'll introduce you to two of my boys, Greg and Rick. I'd like to see them with a nice girl."

Libby almost burst out laughing at the idea of dating one of her brothers. "I'd rather settle in first," she murmured.

"You want to fix her up with Greg?" Cyn rolled her eyes. "He may be your son, Marie, but we both know his only love is that new 4x4 pickup of his. Look how he's out there every Saturday washing and waxing it. I heard one of the times he dated Heidi Potter he almost made her get out and walk from the Railroad Tavern since she had some mud on her shoes."

Libby edged her way to the door. "I'm happy to meet you, too, Marie," she murmured. "Cyn, I'll see you later."

The women were still good-naturedly arguing about Greg's love for his truck as Libby crept out of the kitchen. She didn't breathe a sigh of relief until she was in the blessed silence of her apartment.

What she noticed first when she stepped inside was the temperature; the room was comfortably warm. The second thing she noticed was Matthias seated in the armchair. He held a glass of wine cupped in one hand.

"Do you really enjoy running after those little terrors?" he asked as he took a sip. "Oh, I'm sorry. Would you care for a glass?"

"Yes, thank you." She was curious to see how he would conjure up her wine. She should have known better. She blinked and a glass of wine stood on the coffee table. "I suppose the heat was your idea."

"I thoroughly dislike cold weather." He waved his glass to a tune that might have been silent in his head, but was soon heard by Libby. "I've always found Vivaldi relaxing."

Libby dropped her purse on the couch and sat down. She picked up the glass of wine. She slipped off her shoes and stretched her legs out so her feet could rest on the coffee table.

"Why are you here?"

He cast his eyes skyward. "I thought you would have wished to converse further on your seeing Tyler."

"Oh really? What was I supposed to say— 'Hello, Tyler. In another dimension, I was your wife'? He would have laughed at me." She sipped the wine, enjoying the inner warmth the alcohol gave her. "Why did he act as if he was God's gift to women? He's not the Tyler I know. Not the Tyler I grew up with. He's too arrogant."

"He didn't have you with him all these years. You were his softening feature, Libby. He always loved you. He wanted to be the perfect man for you and he did everything possible to be that man."

"I didn't want Tyler to be something he's not," she said, distressed. "I always loved him just the way he was."

Matthias cocked his head to one side, watching her with his direct gaze. "And what is so wrong in finding out what this Tyler might offer you?"

His smile should have warned her she was in for a surprise that might be very unwelcome. But she was too distracted by the jaunty knock on the door.

She got up and walked over to the door. A quick peek through the curtains told her what she needed to know.

"I'm perfectly safe," Tyler announced, holding up his hands. "And I brought dinner." He held up one hand a little higher. It held two white paper bags emblazoned with a popular fast-food-franchise logo.

"I'd say this is the perfect time to find out." Matthias and his wineglass were gone in a blink of an eye.

Chapter Nine

"I thought you might be hungry," Tyler explained when Libby opened the door. "Hope you like cheeseburgers." He quickly jumped inside before she could change her mind.

Now he could see what she looked like without her bulky coat—and he was highly impressed. She was slender without the anorexic look too many women seemed to prefer nowadays. She didn't wear the bold makeup colors Renee preferred, but her coral lipstick suited her. Her tan wool, pleated skirt ended a couple of inches above her knees, while her orange crewneck sweater skimmed her hips. He noticed her tan leather flats were lying by the couch. She didn't need to be flashy to get a man's attention. She could do it just by being herself.

Dammit, how could one woman be so cute?

He walked into the kitchen and set the bags on the counter. As if he'd been there many times before, he hunted through the cabinets until he found the dishes. In no time, he had emptied the bags and placed food on plates.

"How did you know where I live?" Libby asked, still standing by the door. She only closed it because of the cold air streaming in around her ankles.

"What can I say? It's a small town and it's easy to find out anything you want to know if you know who to ask." He set the two plates on the table. "Ready to eat? I got you the large fries. I wasn't sure, but knowing most women prefer it, I got you Diet Coke."

Libby walked over to the table. "Why the gesture? Because I turned you down for a date?"

She hid her smile as he gallantly pulled out her chair, waited for her to be seated, then carefully pushed it back toward the table.

"You had to eat, didn't you? And since you just moved in, you probably don't have a well-stocked kitchen." Tyler unwrapped his burger and bit into it.

"Oh, and since you've obviously lived here all your life, your kitchen has everything known to man. You know—frozen dinners, cases of beer. All the necessities."

She gingerly lifted the bun to peer at the contents. She was surprised to discover there was no tomato. She had never liked tomatoes on her cheeseburgers and always asked for them to be left off. Libby had few eccentricities, but one was that tomato not even touch her meat.

"Were they out of tomatoes for the burgers?" she asked casually.

A slight frown creased his forehead. "I'm sorry. I don't know why, but I asked for no tomato on your cheeseburger."

"That's fine. I don't like them on my sandwiches." She bit into her cheeseburger and chewed. She picked up her diet drink. "This is a very nice gesture. Thank you."

Tyler's grin reminded her of the Big Bad Wolf right after he huffed and puffed to blow that house down.

"Anything to please a lady." He leaned back in his chair, hooking an arm over the back. "So tell me about Libby Douglas."

She thought for a moment. "Libby Douglas teaches preschoolers."

He shook his head. "No, that's what Libby Douglas does for a living. Not what kind of person she is."

She took a deep breath before beginning her recitation. "Libby Douglas is twenty-nine, has taught preschoolers for five years, enjoys reading, going for walks, poking around antique stores, plays tennis badly and is better at softball and volleyball. She doesn't like people who think too much of themselves or who are unkind to anyone, human or animal.''

"My dog is expecting puppies.''

"All that means is you allowed your dog to get loose at a certain time in her life,'' she replied tartly.

He nodded. "She was very popular that night. Came home tired but happy.''

Libby wondered if this Tyler had a scar behind his knee. She remembered the day he'd had to climb a fence to escape a neighbor's angry German shepherd and wasn't fast enough to elude the animal's sharp teeth.

There were so many questions she ached to ask him, but she wasn't sure she was prepared for his answers.

Instead, she opted to finish her meal.

"So, Libby Douglas, did you leave a loved one behind in Webster Falls?'' he asked. "Someone who might show up at your front door and not understand why I'm here?''

She shook her head. "Not really. But—'' her gaze took on a crafty glimmer, "—Marie Bennett did offer to introduce me to two of her sons.''

Tyler groaned loudly. He leaned forward, waving a french fry at her for emphasis. "That has to be Greg and Rick, and believe me, you don't want anything to do with either of them. They don't know how to treat a lady. While Mrs. Bennett is a great person and their dad a neat guy, Greg and Rick didn't bother learning their lessons.''

She ignored the twinge caused by the mention of her parents. "And you do know how to treat a lady."

"Damn straight." He munched on his french fry and reached for another. "They wouldn't have gotten you the large-size fries, I can tell you that."

"Oh, yes, you are a generous one, aren't you?" Libby dipped her fry in a glob of ketchup. "And what about you? What is there to know about you other than the fact that you're working on the school expansion?" *And you think you're God's gift to women.*

Tyler took a sip of his cola to wash down the fry he'd just eaten. "I've lived here all my life. I went into construction because I like working with my hands. When my dad retired, my parents thought about moving to Arizona, where they'd have milder winters. I didn't want to see the family house go to anyone else, so I offered to buy it from them. I have two brothers and a sister. They're all married and live in the area. I'm thirty, in excellent health, and anyone in town would tell you what a great guy I am." He flashed his wolf's smile again.

"I see. And what would your minister say about you?"

"Well," he hedged, "he would probably tell you a few escapades from my wild youth."

"So since growing up, you've been a model citizen?"

"I can be good when I want to."

Libby felt out of her depth with this Tyler. He obviously enjoyed making women blush. She could feel heat warming her cheeks and only hoped it didn't show. Judging from the look on his face, it did.

She gathered up the food wrappers and stuffed them in the bag. Holding on to that, she stood up, snagging Tyler's empty plate and her own.

"Thank you for dinner," she said in her best schoolteacher's voice. "I hate to be rude and chase you out, but I have lessons to prepare for tomorrow."

Tyler leaned back in his chair and watched her. "C'mon, Teach, what kind of lessons can you come up with for that age? The kids can't be so difficult it would take you all evening to figure out how you'll teach them the alphabet."

"I can see you have no idea what goes on in teaching the young." She gave him a pointed look. "You should be careful, Tyler. They might show you up one day."

He heaved a sigh and pushed himself out of his chair.

"Teach, you are one tough lady." He pulled

his keys out of his jeans pocket and jingled them in his hand. "Don't worry, I'll leave quietly." He strolled toward the door with lazy grace. He opened the door and before walking out, looked over his shoulder and winked. "This time."

The moment the door closed, Libby collapsed against the kitchen counter.

I would say you handled that quite well.

She closed her eyes. "Show yourself. I refuse to talk to the walls."

Matthias appeared the moment she finished speaking. He was seated in the same chair he'd been in earlier.

"Is this better?" He wore pained look of resignation that spoke volumes of what he had to suffer with dealing with humans.

"Yes."

"What do you think of your Tyler?" As Matthias raised his hand, his wineglass reappeared.

"The man here tonight was not my Tyler. He's Renee's Tyler." Libby turned and picked up the dishes, rinsing them before putting them in the dishwasher. "He was obviously hoping for an invitation to spend the night. As if I'd give in *that* easily."

Matthias widened his eyes. "My dear, I am appalled to hear you say that. After all, you teach little ones. That you would actually entertain the idea of having a young man you barely know stay the night is reprehensible.''

"You're talking about the man who happens to be my husband. At least, I always knew him as my husband.'' She wiped off the counters with a damp cloth even though they didn't need it. "I don't like your idea of games, Matthias.''

"This game is yours. If you want to find the Tyler you love then you need to bring him out. You abandoned him, Libby. You left him alone. You never stopped to think that he might have been grieving, too. You didn't want to see how much he needed you to help him work through the loss of your child. You were so engrossed in yourself you never noticed his pain.''

Libby flinched as if he'd struck her.

"And that's why I'm here,'' she whispered. "I wanted a world without them, so here I am in a world basically without me. What I'm finding out is that they didn't need me. Tyler is a freewheeling bachelor instead of a husband with a new house, a mortgage and a grieving wife. My mother has a close friend and lots of outside activities, since she doesn't have any daughters to worry about. Even Miss Regina was able to go on without my being at the school.'' Libby's brow furrowed in pain. "You showed me I really wasn't necessary.''

Matthias held his hand in front of him, examining his nails. "I told you this was a learning experience."

"Then what do I do next?"

"You're a smart girl. You can figure it out." With that, he disappeared.

"It would be nice if you made it easy just once," she muttered.

Not a chance.

TYLER NEVER WORRIED about falling asleep. Usually, he'd fall into bed and be out the second his head hit the pillow.

Tonight he found it more difficult. Because of Libby Douglas. He hadn't planned on stopping off to pick up burgers and take them by her place. And he couldn't remember ever putting in a special order for someone he didn't even know. How could he have known she didn't like tomatoes on her burgers?

He knew it sounded corny, but he viewed her as someone special. She didn't have the flash Renee had. Maybe because she taught rug rats. Her reserve didn't seem to matter, since it suited her so well.

He crossed his hands behind his head and looked up at the ceiling, where he could see shadows chase themselves across the smooth surface.

Even though the air was chilly, he had the window open an inch or so. From outside, he could hear the muted sounds of the Gundersons' collie barking at the Harkers' cat, who enjoyed teasing him by prowling the top of the fence. And it sounded like the Smiths next door were at it again. He swore they only fought so they'd have the pleasure of making up—and they weren't quiet about that, either. He didn't envy them the fighting, but he sure envied them the loving.

His parents were telling him it was time to get married and start a family. They liked to remind him that they'd had their family already started by the time they were Tyler's age. They wanted grandchildren to spoil!

He smiled in the dark. "I bet they'd like Libby."

He already knew what they thought of Renee. While his mother never came right out and revealed her thoughts, the tone of her voice was enough.

"Are you still seeing the Carter girl?" she'd ask every time they talked on the phone.

"Renee and I go out every so often," he'd reply, cautious with his replies. His mother might live out of state, but she was very intuitive. He swore she could read his thoughts even long distance.

"I'm sure there are many nice girls in town you can take out," she'd tell him in her mother-knows-best voice.

Play "Lucky Hearts" and you ge

YOURS
FREE!

**This charming refrigerator magnet looks like a little cherub, a
it's a perfect size for holding notes and recipes. Best of all it's
yours ABSOLUTELY FREE when you accept our NO-RISK offer!**

...then continue your lucky streak
with a sweetheart of a deal!

1. Play Lucky Hearts as instructed on the opposite page.
2. Send back this card and you'll receive brand-new Harlequin American Romance® no
   These books have a cover price of $3.75 each, but they are yours to keep absolutely
3. There's no catch. You're under no obligation to buy anything. We charge nothing—
   ZERO—for your first shipment. And you don't have to make any minimum number
   of purchases—not even one!
4. The fact is thousands of readers enjoy receiving books by mail from the Harlequin
   Reader Service®. They like the convenience of home delivery...they like getting
   the best new novels BEFORE they're available in stores...and they love our
   discount prices!
5. We hope that after receiving your free books you'll want to remain a subscriber. Bu
   choice is yours—to continue or cancel, any time at all! So why not take us up on c
   invitation, with no risk of any kind. You'll be glad you did!

Exciting Harlequin romance novels—FREE!
Plus a Beautiful Cherub Magnet—FREE!

YES!

I have scratched off the silver card. Please send me all the free books and gift for which I qualify. I understand that I am under no obligation to purchase any books, as explained on the back and on the opposite page.

With a coin, scratch off the silver card and check below to see what we have for you.

154 CIH CCPV (U-H-AR-12/97)

HARLEQUIN'S
LUCKY HEARTS
GAME

NAME

ADDRESS   APT.#

CITY   STATE   ZIP

Twenty-one gets you 4 free books, and a free Cherub Magnet!

Twenty gets you 4 free books!

Nineteen gets you 3 free books!

Eighteen gets you 2 free books!

The Harlequin Reader Service®— Here's how it works:

Accepting free books places you under no obligation to buy anything. You may keep the books and g▓ return the shipping statement marked "cancel." If you do not cancel, about a month later we'll send y▓ additional novels and bill you just $3.12 each plus 25¢ delivery per book and applicable sales tax, if a▓ That's the complete price—and compared to cover prices of $3.75 each—quite a bargain! You may c▓ any time, but if you choose to continue, every month we'll send you 4 more books, which you may e▓ purchase at the discount price...or return to us and cancel your subscription.

*Terms and prices subject to change without notice. Sales tax applicable in N.Y.

"Don't worry about me, Mom," he'd reassure her. "You'll have plenty of grandchildren to spoil. I won't let you miss out on that."

Tyler yawned and smiled. "Yeah, she'd like Libby," he whispered before turning over and falling asleep.

Tyler's dreams were never very vivid, but tonight was different. Pictures of Libby floated through his mind.

Strangely enough, she looked to be about five years old, with a cherub's face and smile. She was dressed in a pink dress with ruffles and a little straw hat with a pink ribbon and bow around it. Her shoes were white patent leather and her socks were edged with lace.

Then it seemed five years or so had passed. Her denim shorts were ragged, her T-shirt the same. Her hair was pulled back in a ponytail, but curls escaped to rest against her tanned cheeks and neck. The fishing pole she held explained her tattered appearance. Her smile revealed a missing front tooth.

Next, as a slender teenager with a hint of breast and hips, she was starting to show the picture of femininity she'd grow into. Her sundress was a blue-and-yellow print, her legs tanned and bare. She stood in the middle of a meadow spinning around in a circle, her arms uplifted as if to embrace the sun. The smile on her face rivaled the brightness above.

The sleeping Tyler groaned and turned over, burying his face in his pillow. "Libby," he moaned.

As he slipped deeper into the dream he faced another Libby. A Libby who had reached the full flower of her womanhood. She smiled at him and held out her arms. There was nothing he could do but walk toward her. He knew that if he stayed with her he would find a pleasure he'd never experienced before.

"Tyler." Her voice was a soft whisper. Her skin was like satin against his own.

And her kiss. There was nothing like it.

Then his dream world whirled around him in a sea of fog. She was leaving him! Drifting away!

"No!" He reached for her, but their fingers could barely touch. The look of wistful regret on her face tore through him.

At that very second, Tyler woke up with a violent start. He sat up in bed, feeling sweat pour off his face.

He leaned over and switched on the light. He looked around but couldn't see or hear anything that could have so rudely jerked him awake.

Within minutes, he was asleep again with no memory of his dream.

THE FIRST THING Libby saw the next morning when she arrived at the school was Tyler. He wore a billed cap that was battered and covered with wood dust. He smiled at her and touched his fingers to the bill, then returned to his conversation with the older man standing with him.

Isn't that nice? He remembered you.

"If you don't be quiet I will make sure you never get into the Council of Elders," Libby said under her breath as she smiled back at Tyler.

That's very cruel, Libby.

"You got it."

Might I remind you that I am only here to help you?

"And you need me to get into the council."

"Miss Libby!" Becca ran up and threw her arms around Libby's legs. "King Tut threw up on me when I picked him up after breakfast." She wrinkled her nose in disgust. "It smelled awful and my dress looked really yucky."

"Well, that certainly doesn't sound very nice of him." Libby gave her a hug. "I must say you cleaned up nicely."

The little girl giggled. "Mrs. Robinson said it would have been easier to take me out in the backyard and use the hose on me, but it was too cold. And King Tut ran away cuz he didn't want a bath. Cats hate baths."

Libby smiled at Becca's whispered admission.

"Cats have never liked baths unless they're giving them to themselves," she answered.

Becca took her hand as they walked inside. "Mrs. Robinson said King Tut is old and has a sensitive stomach. I think he did it cuz he doesn't like me. Dogs are better." She looked wistful. "Do you think I will ever get a dog?"

"I'm sure one day you will." Libby stopped by Miss Regina's office to pick up some papers.

"But I can't have a dog at Mrs. Robinson's. I'll have to have a mommy and daddy who will give me a dog." Becca fidgeted with her coat buttons. She looked up. "You would be a good mommy."

Libby looked away from the girl's face. "I hope I will be," she said softly.

"Oh, you will." Becca skipped ahead of her teacher.

"I must say you've made spectacular progress with her."

Libby turned around to face Miss Regina. "Maybe she's finally realized that no one will bite her. Other than Josh, that is."

The older woman smiled at Libby's wry comment. "Today was the first time I saw that little girl smile. She has always been so solemn and withdrawn that I feared she would never come out of her shell. I'm glad to see you were able to draw her out."

"Maybe she thinks of her mother when she sees me," Libby replied.

"Don't get too close, Libby. If Becca's parents can't be found, the authorities might find other relatives. There's no guarantee she'll be able to stay with Mrs. Robinson for much longer. Because of her age, Ada's only called on for short-term foster care."

Libby was stunned by the news. "But right now Becca's only stability is Mrs. Robinson. Taking her away could cause Becca to end up with severe emotional problems. She needs security right now, not being shuffled all over the county."

"That's the way it's done, dear." Miss Regina patted Libby's shoulder. "But for now, we'll just treasure her every day we have her. And perhaps, when that times comes, she'll be able to handle it better."

Dismissed, Libby went on to her classroom. She managed a smile for the children milling around the room. Since they were beginning an art project today, Libby had an aide to assist her. She had met Gwen before, when the young woman was helping with another class.

Libby stood at the front of the room and clapped her hands for attention.

"Let's get our painting smocks on so we can begin our project."

Josh's eyes lit up. "Are we gonna make a mess?"

"No, Josh, we are going to do our best not to make a mess."

As Libby helped fasten the single large button at the back of various paint-smeared cotton smocks, she glanced out the window every so often. She had no desire to check out the weather, either. Instead, she could see the new building going up a short distance away. She could also see the workers. Especially one who appeared to be directing some of the men.

He turned to look at the old school building, especially the row of windows where Libby's classroom was. Even though she wasn't close to the windows, she took a step back when it appeared he was looking straight at her. For good measure she took another step backward, so she knew there was no way he could see her.

But somehow Tyler knew she was there—and actually grinned and winked at her!

Chapter Ten

"So, Teach, where ya goin'?"

Libby turned around and found Tyler striding toward her.

"Since my day is over, I thought I would go home." She leaned against her car door.

"How about some dinner?"

"Oh, I intend to eat dinner." She waited a second. "Alone."

He grinned at her lofty tone. "You don't beat around the bush, do you, Teach?"

"When I want someone to understand what I mean I make it as easy as possible for them." She kept her smile on her lips as she turned around and inserted her key in the door lock. She almost jumped when a gloved hand covered hers.

"Can I ask just one question?"

She looked up to meet his gaze. His eyes lacked their usual cocky arrogance.

"All right."

He paused a moment before speaking. "You're going to hear stories about me. I admit I've been reckless in the past, but there's something about you—" He broke off and took a deep breath. "What I'm saying is, I hope you'll give me a chance."

Libby was surprised and touched by his statement. He sounded sincere.

"So I shouldn't listen to any of the many stories circulating about the wild Tyler Barnes," she said.

He shook his head.

"Or the rumors that you are already very close to a certain woman. I don't believe in poaching on another woman's property."

He could feel those ribbons starting to tie him up and he panicked.

"It's not an exclusive relationship."

"Maybe it isn't to you, but I've heard differently," Libby said. "I wouldn't dream of demanding you give her up. I'm just saying that I've never enjoyed being part of a crowd." She reached for the door handle. "Good night, Tyler."

He could tell there was no trying to reason with her right now. He stepped back and allowed her to pull her door open and climb into her car.

"I'm not going to give up, Libby."

She finished fastening her seat belt before she

looked up at him. "Something tells me you're not the type to give up, Tyler. And I'm sure it's a trait that's stood by you for a lot of years. But I'd like a chance to get settled before you start your chasing. Fair enough?"

He grinned, clearly back to his old self. "You got it." He touched two fingers to his cap in a salute and sauntered off.

Libby watched Tyler walk away. If nothing else, she could enjoy the way his body moved as he walked.

"I know I'm in big trouble now."

Why didn't you just jump the man while you had him in your clutches?

Libby started up the engine. "And why don't you keep your opinions to yourself?"

Pleased with herself for having the last word, she drove off.

"YOU HAVE TO GET OUT and meet people," Bonnie insisted the moment she had Libby on the phone. As soon as she'd suggested that Libby go out with her and her husband that evening, Libby had started making her excuses. Unfortunately, they sounded as weak to Bonnie as they did to Libby. "I'm not letting you get out of this, Libby. We'll be by to pick you up at seven."

"Bonnie!" Oh no, she was whining. She hated whining. Especially when she was the whiner.

"See you at seven. And be ready!" Bonnie hung up before Libby could come up with any more excuses.

Libby dropped the phone in the cradle and slumped against the kitchen counter.

"An evening out will do you a world of good."

Libby looked over the counter. Matthias was comfortably seated in what she was starting to call "his" chair.

"Why? I'm already resigned to the fact that I'll still be here when I'm an old lady. And Tyler will marry and have children—" she gulped, her voice catching on the last word "—with someone else. So why don't you just go make another person's life hell."

His eyes widened. "My dear, I would never consign you to such a horrible place. Go out this evening with your friends. When was the last time you've gone out and enjoyed yourself?"

Libby looked down at the floor. It was easier to count the tiles than to answer him.

"That long, hmm? Then you truly need to go out. And being the gentleman I am, I will leave so you can prepare yourself."

As always, he was gone in the blink of an eye.

"He wants to run my life," she muttered, pushing herself away from the counter.

She dragged her feet as she walked into the

bedroom. She stopped short when she noticed pieces of clothing lying across the end of the bed.

"Matthias, you are a very sneaky individual."

She picked up the denim skirt and held it against her. The first thing she noticed was that it ended several inches above the knee. The red-and-white gingham blouse had a silky feel to it and the collar was edged with lace. A pair of red cowboy boots completed the ensemble.

A twinge of excitement started deep in her stomach. "I can do it," she whispered, heading for the bathroom.

After she finished her shower, she took her time with her makeup. When she was done, she stood back feeling pleased with the final results. She'd used a smoky green eye shadow with a touch of gray to lend mystery to her eyes. A hint of bronzy rose blush added color to her cheeks, and she wore a matching color on her lips.

Needless to say, she discovered her new outfit fit her perfectly, showing her legs off to their best advantage. The red boots felt as comfortable as an old pair of slippers.

"Obviously, you were determined I'd get out tonight," she said out loud. "Why? Are you planning a party here? Will I come home to an entity orgy?"

You should be ashamed for even thinking such a thing.

"Are you trying to say entities don't have a sex life?" She found herself curious to know more about these beings that seem to enjoy dropping in and interfering with mortal lives.

We do not interfere. We strive to make lives better.

"Says you."

She glanced at the window when she heard the sound of a motor, to see a red Blazer pulling up by the stairs.

"Be good, Matthias. Don't make any long-distance phone calls. Or intergalaxy phone calls, or whatever you'd call them." She grabbed her purse and ran out the door.

Please do not try to be amusing. It doesn't suit you.

"YOU LOOK GREAT!" Bonnie gushed as Libby climbed into the back seat. "And here I haven't seen my feet in weeks!"

"I don't know why she worries," Gary, Bonnie's husband, said. "They're still there."

Bonnie rolled her eyes. "You can tell he has a lot of sympathy for me, can't you?"

"You're not the one who has to go out at midnight to find brownie-chunk ice cream."

"Cravings are very important to a pregnant woman," Libby told him.

"Maybe, but why do they always show up in

the middle of the night?'' He backed down the driveway, honking a greeting when Cyn appeared at the back door and waved at them. He glanced at his wife. ''Cyn didn't want to go out with us tonight?''

Bonnie shook her head. ''She said she was going to relax with a good book, but I think she has a hot date and doesn't want us to know.''

Gary raised his eyebrows. ''Oho. Raymond?''

''He was last month.''

''Then who?''

She flashed an impish grin. ''Harold Lutz.''

''Harold Lutz? That's a joke, right? He's not at all her type.'' He shook his head, then looked into the rearview mirror toward Libby. ''In case you haven't guessed, Cyn is the town's wild woman. She figures her age shouldn't hold her back.''

''She's also said she doesn't want to get married again because divorce is a nuisance and she doesn't want to bury anyone she loves,'' Bonnie explained. ''She had been going out with Raymond for about three months, but she said the bells just weren't ringing for her, so she said goodbye to him and hello to Harold.''

Gary laughed. ''Poor Harold. He'll never have a peaceful moment now.''

''Bonnie, are you going to tell me where we're going, or am I supposed to trust you?''

"We're going to the Outpost," she replied. "Part of it is a restaurant and the rest is a bar and dance floor. They always have great bands there. They don't play just country and western, either. Most of the bands also play a lot of rock and roll." She grimaced. "I'm not supposed to dance until after the baby comes, but I can sit there and listen to the music. Ha! There's no fun in that."

"So she pushes me onto all the 'unavailable' women to dance," Gary interjected. "I'm not allowed to go anywhere near a woman who's truly available. Bonnie's promised to sit on anyone who gets too close to me."

"I did not say that!" She punched him in the arm. "I just said I'd make them sorry for coming close to my honey," she cooed.

Libby laughed at Bonnie's antics, but a part of her felt regret as she recalled similar byplay she used to share with Tyler.

There had been a lot of Friday and Saturday nights when they had gone out for dinner and dancing. They both enjoyed dancing, especially when they were in each other's arms.

That was when a disturbing thought occurred to her. What if Tyler was there with Renee? Libby shifted in her seat and wondered if she could think up a logical excuse to go back home.

Then it was too late. Gary pulled into a partially filled parking lot and stopped the car. He walked around the front to help Bonnie down, then assisted Libby.

"I have no sense of balance," Bonnie confessed. "Actually, I feel like one of those blow-up punching clowns. If you try to tip me I'll just rock back and forth on my feet." She laughed.

Libby put her arm around Bonnie's shoulders to console her. "Think how you'll feel when you can see your feet again."

"More like how I'll feel when I don't have to visit the bathroom every five minutes or have the kid playing basketball inside my belly." She grimaced as she rubbed her taut abdomen. "I swear he hears every word I say and gets even with me one way or another."

Libby smiled, remembering the days of never seeing her feet. Of wondering if she would ever get past the morning sickness. Of wondering if she would ever have another peaceful night's sleep without the baby turning somersaults. Of course, there had been no peaceful night of sleep after Sara was born, either, since she'd seemed to enjoy waking her parents up several times a night. Libby was still smiling as she realized she was thinking about her daughter and not feeling the shafts of pain she usually felt. She had an idea she might be finally healing.

Gary opened the door for the women. The minute they stepped inside, loud music assaulted their eardrums.

Libby looked around. It was the same as she remembered—even the bartenders and waitresses. She saw many familiar people and grieved that they didn't know her. For a moment she wanted to run away.

You aren't the type of woman to run away. You'll fight for what you want, Libby.

She made a face. *Thanks a lot.*

"Isn't it great?" Bonnie shouted over the music. Her eyes were bright with excitement as she bounced to the beat, looking a little like a colorful penguin with her waddle.

"I'll tell you after I get my hearing back," Libby shouted back in reply, getting a grip on her fear and pushing it down.

"C'mon, I found us a table." Gary took each woman's hand and led them over to an unoccupied table. "What do you want?" he asked Libby.

She wrinkled her nose as she thought about it. "Whatever beer they have on tap. I'm not too fussy."

He nodded, then looked at Bonnie.

She sighed. "I know, I know. I can't have beer or wine, so I guess I'll settle for club soda."

Gary bent down and kissed her lightly on the lips. "I'll let you be designated driver."

"You try driving with the steering wheel jamming into your belly and see how you feel about it,'' she retorted. ''Go get our drinks, slave.''

Gary performed a mock salaam and sauntered off.

''I'd say you have a real sweetheart.'' Libby leaned over so Bonnie could hear her more easily.

She smiled and nodded. ''I like to remind him how lucky he is to have me.'' She and Libby chuckled.

''How did you meet him?''

''We've known each other since our first day in Miss Regina's preschool. Gary once told me he fell in love with me that day. It took me a few more days, but we've been together since then. We tried dating other people in high school, but it didn't work out. We always went back to each other.''

The roar in Libby's ears sounded like a tornado. She was positive she was sitting in a wind tunnel.

Bonnie and Gary had met in preschool. There had never been anyone else for either of them.

''When did you get married?'' she asked in a faint voice.

Luckily, Bonnie didn't notice her pallor. ''Six years ago. We wanted some time to ourselves before starting our family. And now—'' she patted her rounded tummy ''—we're starting out with the acrobat here.''

"You're very lucky." Libby blinked rapidly to keep back her tears.

Bonnie looked at her and was about to say something when Gary showed up holding three glasses.

"Here you go, ladies. Tips are gratefully accepted." He set a frosty glass filled with beer in front of Libby and an ice-filled club soda in front of Bonnie.

"Don't worry, honey. I'll tip you later." Bonnie winked at him.

"She only has me around as a sex slave," Gary confided to Libby. He adopted a mournful expression.

"I'd say you're not suffering all that much," Libby teased. She picked up her glass and sipped her beer.

"Gary, my love, take Libby out there and dance with her," Bonnie ordered.

"Bonnie, you don't have to—"

"All right, lady, let's show 'em how it's done." Gary grabbed Libby's hand and pulled her out of her chair.

Libby didn't have a chance to protest. Gary proved to be a dancer who kept her frantically remembering the steps. By the time the music stopped she was out of breath.

She laughed as Gary swung her around when a new tune began. "Not again!"

"Yes again. Hell, I usually can't dance with a good-looking woman without Bonnie getting her hackles up." He grinned, holding her hand over her head as he directed her in a fancy spin that made her short skirt flare even higher.

"I'm glad to know I'm considered safe." Libby laughed again, not only because for some reason she found Gary's comment funny, but also because she was finding out she was enjoying herself.

The people around her on the dance floor, the lively music and Gary keeping up with her step for step was freeing something inside her.

One more twirl sent her spinning, and when she slowed, she saw a familiar figure walking into the club. With another equally familiar person in tow. Libby froze for a moment, watching Tyler look for a table. Then he zeroed in on her. For one brief second there was no one else in the room as they stared at each other.

Then Renee touched Tyler's arm to point out an empty table and the moment was lost. Libby was back in Gary's arms, and all too soon the music stopped.

Libby would have preferred to stay out on the dance floor where she felt safe, but Gary started escorting her back.

"Thank you," she told him.

"No, thank *you.*"

Libby looked at their table and saw Bonnie talking to a young woman. Libby recognized her as a clerk who worked at the post office, but pretended never to have seen her before.

"Oh please." Gary moaned. He leaned closer to Libby. "That's Liza Kelly. She has no idea what dancing is about. She has two left feet, is tone deaf and likes to sing while she stomps all over my toes."

"There's my honeybun," Bonnie cooed when they approached the table. "Honey, Liza's been dying to dance with you."

Gary managed a pained smile. "Sure. Liza?"

The woman, whose complexion could be called pasty at best, brightened up. "I'd love to, Gary."

"Liza, this is Libby Douglas. She's taking my place at Miss Regina's," Bonnie said. "Libby, this is Liza Kelly."

"Pleased to meet you," the woman said shyly.

"C'mon, Liza, let's burn up that floor." Gary took her hand and led her out to the dance floor.

Bonnie's and Libby's eyes met.

"I know, it's really mean," Bonnie said without apology, "but Liza wouldn't have a chance to dance if Gary didn't dance with her first. She's too shy to just go up to a man and ask him to dance like a lot of the single women will do."

"Did you ever stop to think it might have something to do with her two left feet?"

"Good thing Gary's wearing his boots."

The two women laughed.

Libby picked up her glass and sipped the cold brew. She realized if she sat at an angle, she could see Tyler without appearing to watch him.

"Well, well, well."

Libby looked at Bonnie. "What?"

"It appears you've caught someone's interest."

Libby shook her head. She doubted anyone would notice her that quickly. "Don't tell me. He looks like a horse and dances like one, too."

Bonnie leaned across the table. "Not this one. He's tall, dark and very good-looking—a prime catch in this town. A lot of women have been trying to reel him in since high school."

Libby leaned forward in turn. "If he's that great why is he available?"

"Maybe it's because the right woman hasn't thrown her line in the pool yet." Bonnie's grin broadened. "And he's coming this way."

Libby didn't have to turn around to know Bonnie was talking about Tyler. Nor did she need an announcement to know he was walking her way.

Every nerve in her body was vibrating more wildly the closer he came.

"So, Teach, are you brave enough to dance with me?"

Chapter Eleven

Libby looked up. To her surprise, she didn't see the man she expected after her previous meetings with him. Tyler had lost a little of his arrogance. His grin was infectious and cocky, but she could read a hint of uncertainty in his eyes. As if he thought she might refuse his invitation.

Which she considering doing. For about half a second.

"Thank you, I'd love to." She stood up and took his outstretched hand.

Tyler's look of relief was immediate. He led her back to the dance floor and turned to face her.

Libby felt the butterflies in her stomach turn into army tanks. Tyler placed her arms around his neck and braced his hands at the base of her spine, bringing her flush against his body.

Libby caught her breath as she felt the heat of his body flow through hers and the woodsy spice scent of his aftershave prick her nostrils. It was the smell she always associated with him. She wanted to lean even closer against him, to nestle her cheek against the curve of his neck, to just experience him.

"You smell like spring," he murmured against her hair.

She wanted to cry. How many times had he said that exact same thing when they danced? She cleared her throat to dislodge the lump residing there.

"I never thought of myself smelling like a season." She closed her eyes against the flood of memories as she spoke words she'd said many times before. "But I guess smelling like spring is better than smelling like winter."

His chuckle seemed to vibrate against her cheek.

"It's not so bad, is it?"

Libby tipped her head back so she could see him. "What isn't?"

"Dancing with me."

"I won't consider it torture as long as you don't step on my toes."

His dark eyes glinted with humor. "I'll do my best." His palm cupped her head and brought it back to rest against his shoulder.

Libby noticed Renee Carter standing at the bar, her back turned to it so she could watch the dancers. Libby and Tyler, in particular. There was no mistaking the fury written on her face. She obviously didn't like what she was seeing.

I was right. She still has thick thighs.

Uncharitable thoughts, Libby.

Uncharitable? It's more like a statement of fact!

When the music stopped, Libby started to pull away. But just as quickly, another song began and Tyler merely tightened his hold on her.

"There's no way I'm letting go of you so soon," he murmured in her ear.

She shivered at the touch of his lips against her skin.

"Don't you think your date would have something to say about that?" Her gaze was locked with Renee's. Libby felt as if she should erect an invisible shield against the other woman's deadly glare.

His chest rose and fell with the deep breath he took.

"You don't poach," he said, recalling her words.

"That's right."

"And I told you, I belong to me." His lips brushed against her ear. "I dance with whom I please."

She looked up. "But etiquette should remind you that you did bring another lady."

His eyes bored into hers. "Then why do I go to sleep thinking about you?"

Libby unconsciously moistened her lips. Tyler's eyes darkened with fire.

Mercifully, the music ended. Libby pulled away and this time Tyler willingly released her. He started to follow her back to her table.

"No," she said in a low voice, "it's better if I go alone."

Libby walked back to the table, where Bonnie sat with a curious look on her face. Gary was also watching her. With every step, she felt Tyler's gaze following her.

"And here I didn't think you knew anyone," Bonnie whispered furiously once Libby dropped into her chair.

"He helped me out when my car wouldn't start," she replied, picking up her glass of beer and draining it.

"I hate to tell you this, but Renee Carter believes she has Tyler all wrapped up, and she doesn't appreciate any other woman dancing with him."

"Oh hell." Gary groaned and nodded to indicate someone approaching their table. "Angry woman at twelve o'clock."

"Just who do you think you are?"

Libby mentally straightened her backbone before she looked up. Renee was dressed in a pair of denim shorts that barely covered the essentials and a blue-and-white blouse that tied just under her breasts.

"I think I am someone who is sitting here with her friends. And I don't believe I know you."

Renee's mascara-coated lashes seemed to bat fast enough to cause a breeze. "Tyler Barnes is mine," she stated between clenched teeth. "I suggest you stay away from him."

Libby's eyes shifted a fraction to see a grim-faced Tyler bearing down on them. She felt anger flare within her. With her calm and happy nature, Libby was rarely angry. She never found it beneficial. But now she found it very cleansing. The man who should be her husband was with another woman. And this woman was blatantly putting her brand on him.

Fine, Libby thought to herself. But she wasn't going to make it easy for her.

"Then I suggest you get your boyfriend a collar and tag with your name printed on it so everyone will know." She deliberately raised her voice just enough that Tyler and anyone within earshot would hear her.

Renee's face turned tomato red with mingled embarrassment and fury.

"Major mistake, darlin'." Tyler's drawl came from behind her.

Renee turned and must have seen enough in his expression to know he spoke the truth.

"I asked the lady to dance because she's new in town and doesn't know many people. Although it isn't any of your business why I asked her." His low voice was deadly calm. "Why don't we go back to our table?"

Renee flashed one last glare at Libby before spinning around on her high heels and tottering after Tyler. Her words were drowned out by the music, which mercifully started up again.

"Renee seemed a bit testy," Bonnie observed. She turned to her husband and smiled. "Sweetie, would you get us another drink?"

Gary rolled his eyes. "I always miss out on the good stuff." With a loud groan, he stood up and ambled over to the bar.

Bonnie leaned over so Libby wouldn't have to strain her ears. "Tyler Barnes was very much the class hunk all through high school. A lot of us knew Renee Carter wanted Tyler, but for some crazy reason she kept him dangling. After graduation, she left town and got married. After her divorce, she moved back, and the first guy to take her out was Tyler. She's been trying to land him ever since." Bonnie's expression showed concern. "What I'm saying, Libby, is I don't want to see you hurt."

Libby reached for her hand and squeezed it.

"Thank you for caring, Bonnie. It was easy to tell right off that he likes to play the field. I wouldn't allow someone like that to play with my feelings."

Bonnie didn't seem convinced. "If you had sat here and seen the way you and he looked out there, you'd be saying something else." She glanced up and noticed her husband making his way toward them.

Libby felt pain inside because she knew Bonnie was right. This Tyler wasn't the one she loved so deeply. But out there on the dance floor, she'd felt a hint of the man she had known.

What are you going to do about it, Libby? Find a way to bring that part of his nature out into the open?

Go away, Matthias.

Don't be rude.

She smiled and accepted her drink.

Libby soon found herself to be a much-sought-after dance partner. In an attempt to convince Bonnie she had misinterpreted what had happened between Libby and Tyler on the dance floor, she accepted every invitation.

Bonnie seemed to think Libby was enjoying herself, which relieved Libby to no end. In reality, she spent the night on edge, and purposely not looking in Tyler and Renee's direction. The last thing she wanted was to witness the other woman's triumph.

BY THE TIME Bonnie and Gary dropped her off at her apartment, Libby was pleasantly tired.

"Thank you for inviting me along," she told the couple.

"This will be probably the last time we'll be able to get out, so thank you for going with us." Bonnie smiled. "If you need anything, you call, all right?"

She nodded, then waved and walked up the stairway to her door.

Once inside, Libby dropped her purse on the coffee table and went into the bedroom. Even though she'd kept the lights off, she could easily navigate her way around the furniture.

As she discarded her clothing, Libby felt an overwhelming weariness overtake her.

She shouldn't be here alone! Tyler should be here with her.

Ah, but when was the last time she and Tyler had gone to bed together? When was the last time they had made love?

Her mind voiced and answered the questions at the same time.

She had walled herself off from Tyler after Sara's death. She hadn't wanted comfort from her husband. She hadn't wanted anyone to comfort her.

Still holding her blouse in her hands, she abruptly sat on the side of the bed. She had deliberately kept the truth from herself.

She didn't want comfort because she blamed herself. She ordinarily had checked her baby several times during the night, but that night she had been so exhausted she hadn't woken up once.

And her baby had died alone.

Sobs ripped their way up Libby's throat and spilled from her lips. She clutched her blouse against her chest as if it were a security blanket. The tears streamed down her cheeks and dripped unheeded onto the cotton material. She bent at the waist while the pain rolled through her body. She had no idea how long she cried. She didn't care. The tears didn't ease her pain. All they did was give her proof she had been lying to herself for too long.

When her crying started to subside, Libby slowly got up, moving woodenly as she pulled out a nightgown and finished undressing.

With her face scrubbed clean and her body encased in a soft flannel nightgown, Libby lay under the covers. She shivered. A coldness was within her and there wasn't any form of warmth that could take that chill away.

The doctors told me over and over it wasn't my

fault. They said it could have happened at any time. It's one of those unexplained mysteries. They still know little about SIDS. They said I shouldn't worry about it happening again. I shouldn't obsess about it. I need to think of Tyler. What he's feeling now.

Her thoughts ran rampant through her mind. The words tumbled over each other as she slowly but surely made sense of them.

Congratulations, Libby. You're on your way to forgiving yourself.

As Matthias's words echoed in her mind, she fell asleep.

LIBBY WOKE UP to the sound of insistent tapping at her front door.

"Oh Cyn," she moaned, crawling out of bed. "I really don't want to tell you all about my evening now." She pushed her hair away from her face. She stumbled across the room and soon reached the door. "Please, Cyn." She opened the door and, to her shock, faced Tyler.

"I guess Cyn's still asleep." He pointed his thumb over his shoulder. "May I come in?"

Speechless at seeing the last person she'd expected to find on her doorstep, Libby stepped back.

Tyler moved inside and closed the door behind him. He leaned against it with his hands behind him. His crooked smile was barely visible in the darkness.

"I guess you weren't expecting me."

"I was asleep," she muttered, stating the obvious. Her sleep-fogged brain was having trouble assimilating that this wasn't a wishful dream on her part.

"Yeah, I gathered that." The light might have been almost nonexistent, but the hot glow in his eyes seem to send a shaft of light between them. "You're not going to send me away, are you?"

"I should."

"I wasn't with her tonight, Libby."

"I know."

Her whisper hovered in the air between them as Tyler looked at her in confusion.

Her smile was brief. "I would have smelled her perfume on you," she explained.

Tyler took one step forward. So did Libby. Another step and they were in each other's arms.

Libby felt as if she had come home. His embrace was so familiar to her, she wanted to cry. Instead, she tightened her arms around his neck and nestled her cheek against the curve of his shoulder.

Tyler's kisses were butterfly soft against her forehead and cheeks, but no less thrilling for their tenderness. She found the taste of his skin slightly salty and rough under her tongue as she refamiliarized herself with everything about him.

How long had it been since they held each other this way? How long had it been since they had well and truly kissed?

She tipped her head back, baring her throat to his mouth, which zeroed in on the soft skin there.

"Tyler," she whispered.

"Libby." He made her name sound like a prayer. His arms tightened around her as he picked her up and cradled her against his chest. "Don't say no." He brushed his mouth against hers. "Please."

If he had behaved like the cocksure rebel he'd been acting like before, she would have pushed him out the door and locked it behind him. But he begged her, sincerity ringing in his voice. He held her as if she were a fragile package that required delicate handling. He didn't arrogantly head for the bedroom as if anticipating his welcome. He waited for her to make the decision.

She couldn't keep him in suspense for long. Not when her own body was quivering like a tightly strung bow.

"Yes."

The word was so softly spoken that even with their mouths a breath apart, he shouldn't have been able to hear her. But he did. He groaned softly and pressed his forehead against hers. What had started on the dance floor would finish here.

Tyler carried Libby into the bedroom and carefully placed her on the rumpled bedcovers.

Libby brushed his hands away from his shirt front and released the buttons herself. With each button unfastened, she pressed her lips against another inch of bared skin. With her hands pressed flat against his chest, she felt his muscles tense under her touch. When his shirt hung open, she worked on the waistband button on his jeans. She smiled at the bulge under the zippered fly and pressed her palm there.

Tyler drew in a sharp breath and hissed a word that could have been a curse or a prayer.

"It appears you're somewhat tense, Mr. Barnes," Libby whispered, still keeping her palm pressed against him. She could feel the heat coming from him as she slowly lowered the zipper. His white cotton briefs contrasted with the dark material of his jeans.

"You could call it that." Beads of sweat popped out on his forehead. He reached down to unbutton the three buttons at the throat of her nightgown, then grasped the fabric at her knees and carefully pulled upward. She shifted her body to allow him to pull the gown over her head.

Within seconds, his shirt, jeans and boots were lying on the floor along with her nightgown.

Libby looked up as she slid back onto the bed. She didn't say a word. She didn't have to. All she needed to do was hold out her hand to him.

Tyler leaned forward, resting one bent knee on the bed as he allowed her to pull him toward her. He gathered her into his arms and kissed her slowly and deeply until they both were out of breath.

As she ran her hands over his shoulders and down his hard, muscled arms, he was drawing light circles around the curve of her breast.

"So sweet," he muttered, trailing his mouth across the taut peak. He closed his mouth around her nipple and suckled.

Libby cried out as lightning shot through her body from her breast, to her center. As Tyler's mouth feasted on her breast, his hands were equally busy trailing along her belly to her thighs. His fingers roamed down her legs to her knees and then slowly back up, but he deliberately ignored the area she hungered for him to touch. She whimpered, twisting under the sensual play of his fingertips. She dug her nails into his shoulders as punishment, but he merely laughed and continued his tantalizing caresses.

This Tyler didn't realize Libby had a few tricks up her nonexistent sleeve. She dragged her fingertips across his chest, tangling them in the crisp hair there, then continued a path downward.

The white cotton briefs were pushed down and her hand closed firmly and warmly around his erection. His head snapped upward and eyes gleaming white-hot bored into hers.

"You don't play fair, Teach."

Libby smiled. She was secure in her sensuality with this man and she intended to show him all.

"Oh, I play fair as long as I win." She squeezed gently, sliding her hand slowly downward, then back up.

Tyler gasped at her intimate touch.

"Just a minute."

He was off the bed and rummaging through his jeans pockets until he found what he wanted. He was back before Libby had a chance to consider what she was doing.

He loomed over her like a conqueror, but instead of the swift and deep thrust she expected, he entered her slowly. She stared into his eyes, watching the pupils contract as she tightened around him.

Tyler felt as if he was drowning in a velvet sheath that fit him as if it was custom made. He felt as if he'd come home. He doubted any other woman could make him feel as he did now. And as his movements increased and he felt her legs curve over his and her hips rise up to meet him, he knew he could now die a very happy man.

Chapter Twelve

Tyler was positive he had died and gone to heaven.

He should have been lying back, feeling sated and smug. That was what he usually felt for about five minutes, before he started getting antsy and ready to leave a warm bed and head for his own home. Normally, he didn't feel comfortable spending the night in a woman's bed. Not even Renee's.

He told himself he should be climbing out of bed right now and pulling on his clothes instead of lying here with a sleeping Libby in his arms. Except he wasn't eager to relinquish her and leave the silky softness of her body. Holding her seemed so right. She curled against him as if she had been made for him, and his arms wrapped around her instinctively.

Their mingled scent was sharp in his nostrils. Tyler found himself curious to explore her bathroom. To find out what she used to make her hair smell so exotic—was that almond?—while the rest of her smelled like spring. He rubbed his chin across the top of her head so he could feel the silky softness of her hair.

Come on, Libby! Say yes. I'll even stand on my head if you say you'll go steady with me.

Tyler frowned as the odd words rang through his mind. Why would they sound so real, as if he'd actually spoken them? He'd never gone steady in his life!

Libby murmured something indistinguishable and stirred in his arms.

"I'm sorry," she said softly, raising herself slightly on one arm.

"I was afraid you considered me pretty boring company," he teased. He used his fingers to brush an unruly lock of hair off her face. He carefully tucked it behind her ear, his fingers lingering at the delicate shell.

His eyes were accustomed to the darkness, so he could easily see her face. But it was her eyes that caught his attention—and a question in them that he felt he should know the answer to. What was she trying to tell him?

Libby looked past him.

"I think you should leave now," she said softly.

He sat up so quickly she had to lean back so

she wouldn't slip backward. The corner of the sheet covering her breasts started to slide downward until she grabbed hold of it.

He told himself he had heard wrong. "Are you kicking me out?"

"Yes, I am." She nodded as she said the words, as if to make sure he didn't misunderstand her blunt request. As if he could have!

Tyler rubbed his hand over his chin. The skin was bristly to the touch.

"I thought you might want to cook me breakfast in the morning. If we decide to get up in time, that is." He raised his eyebrows.

She didn't laugh or blush at his provocative remark.

"I'm sure you can find something for breakfast at your own home or at any restaurant in town," she said in an even voice.

Libby slipped out of bed and walked around to the other side. She picked up her nightgown and slid it over her head.

Tyler felt regret when her nude body was covered with lilac print flannel. Before he could say something, his own clothes were dropped on his bare stomach. He sat up and pulled his shirt on, then tugged on his briefs.

"Some hostess you are, darlin'."

The light in the bathroom sent a wide beam across the carpet as Libby disappeared into the room. A moment later, she reappeared with a hair-brush in her hand. She ran it through her hair, smoothing the locks he had combed his fingers through not all that long ago.

"You got what you came for. Now you can go home feeling like a victor." She set the brush down on the dresser and walked toward the door-way.

Tyler hurriedly pulled on his jeans, zipping and buttoning as he followed Libby into the living room. He carried his boots in one hand.

"What's wrong, Libby?" He remained on her heels as she strode into the kitchen and took a glass out of a cabinet. She filled it with water and drank thirstily.

"Nothing." She set the now-empty glass down, then turned around and leaned against the counter.

"Then you tell me why after the most incred-ible sex two people could share, you're throwing me out." He walked toward her until their bodies almost touched.

She reached behind her and flipped on the light. The bright glare caused them both to blink rap-idly.

"Yes, the sex was incredible." Her lips curled slightly. "But I need more than just that, Tyler. You can have sex with anyone. It's the meeting of souls that counts. Good night, Tyler."

He felt anger bristling along his spine. "Fine.

If that's the way you see it, fine," he snapped, haphazardly tucking his shirt into his jeans. "Good night to you, too."

He stalked out, but even with his temper raging, he took great care not to slam the front door as he left.

Libby gripped the counter so tightly her knuckles were white.

We have a meeting of souls, Libby. That's what our lovemaking is. There's a hell of a lot more than just sex between us.

"He didn't even recognize the words."

Her whisper hung heavily in the air as she slowly made her way back to bed. Not to sleep, but to grieve over what she had wanted so badly and what she had actually received.

DAMMIT! He sure showed her, hadn't he? She tried to say that the sex they'd had wasn't all that important. Then she'd thrown him out! Fine. She could just sleep alone from now on. He wasn't going to put himself in that situation again.

But then he remembered that flannel nightgown covering her from throat to toes. It looked like some flower-covered sack, but damm, she still looked so sexy with her drowsy features and sleepy eyes. How come he was getting aroused just thinking about her?

Tyler pounded the dashboard in frustration.

"Why did she have to make things so complicated?" he growled, pressing down harder on the accelerator. Then he eased off. The last thing he wanted was a ticket for speeding.

He parked his truck in the garage and walked into the house.

Tyler grimaced when he noticed the message light blinking madly on his answering machine. He had a pretty good idea who'd left messages, but hell, he'd always been a glutton for punishment.

"Tyler, baby, I'm sorry if I said something wrong tonight. Come on, sweetie, talk to your Renee."

"Tyler, honey, are you really mad at me? It was just that that woman was making eyes at you and I was jealous. Tyler?"

"Tyler, don't be mad at me. In fact..." she paused, her voice lowered to a seductive purr "...why don't you come on over so we can make up?"

"Damn you to hell, Tyler Barnes! No one treats me like this. You are slime! Do you hear that, you bastard?"

Tyler winced at the earsplitting shriek coming from the answering machine. He quickly shut it off.

"I'm surprised she didn't blow out all the circuits," he muttered, heading for the bedroom.

His usual practice was to take a shower before going to sleep. This time he just stripped off his clothing and climbed into bed. Libby's scent was still on his skin and he decided he liked it. A lot.

"I'm not giving her another thought," he muttered, punching his pillow into a pleasing shape and burrowing into it. "Not one more thought."

Except, as he fell asleep, he remembered just how sweet she tasted.

IT HAD TAKEN LIBBY most of the morning just to get out of bed. She huddled under the covers and stared at the wall.

I'm surprised you're not jumping up and down with happiness.

"Oh sure, I'm just ecstatic."

Sarcasm, dear Libby?

Her upper lip curled. "Sarcasm is the least of it. Let's just say the man was happy because he'd had the best sex ever."

Matthias's figure wavered in shadow, then appeared in front of her.

"Oh dear. I'd say he didn't choose the right words."

She glared at him, but along with her anger her expression revealed sorrow and pain.

"I don't care what I'm supposed to do. I don't care what he's supposed to do. I want to go back.'' Tears caused her voice to come out a bit fuzzy.

Matthias leaned back in his chair, pressing his fingertips together. ''Do you truly want to go back to an empty life?''

Those same tears burned her eyes. ''I didn't have an empty life.''

''Didn't you? Libby, you had a husband you ignored, a baby you mourned to the point of obsession, a family you pushed away. Tell me, what else did you have back there?''

She looked away. She refused to meet his eyes in the face of the logic he'd laid out before her.

''And what do I have here? A man who's not my husband, no baby and no family.''

''I would say that you could return, but here you seem to be making more progress in finding out what really matters to you.''

She still looked away. ''And if I go back, Tyler will probably end up with Renee Carter and all she'll do is make him miserable,'' she whispered.

''You have so much love to give, Libby. Open yourself up to the world around you. Remind yourself it isn't a crime to have another child.''

Libby swallowed the lump in her throat. When she looked up again, Matthias was gone. The quiet of her apartment was suddenly too much for her. She went off to shower and dress.

"How was your night out with Bonnie and Gary?" Cyn asked the moment Libby stepped outside. "Did you enjoy yourself?"

She should have known she wouldn't be able to quietly sneak off. Her first horrified thought was that Cyn had seen Tyler's truck parked near the garage, a spot that at least wasn't visible from the street. The last thing she needed was any negative gossip from neighbors. But she didn't want her landlady thinking the worst of her, either.

Cyn's open, friendly smile didn't intimate that she had noticed Tyler's truck.

"What are you doing?" Libby stared at the many boxes Cyn had piled outside the open garage.

"Getting out the Christmas decorations." Cyn put one box on top of another. "I usually get them out right after Thanksgiving, but I'm a week late."

"I didn't realize December was already here," Libby murmured, looking into one open box and seeing a pair of plastic candles that were obviously meant to be set up outside.

"It does creep up fast, doesn't it?" Cyn piled a stack of candy canes. "I line the walkway with these," she explained. "I've always loved the holiday season."

Libby studied the older woman's vivid green

fleece pants and tunic top. A bejewelled Christmas tree was pinned to one shoulder.

The last thing Libby wanted to think about was the holidays. Except, deep down, she could feel a thread of excitement curling upward.

"What will you have the children do for their holiday pageant?" Cyn asked. "Miss Regina always puts on a wonderful pageant for the parents. Each class always does something special."

"I guess I'll decide on Monday." Libby looked at all the boxes, a little chagrined to have forgotten about the coming holiday. "Would you like some help?"

Cyn shook her head. "I love doing this myself. Gary will be over later to put the lights on the house."

Libby stared at several boxes marked Christmas Lights.

"All of these lights go up?"

Cyn nodded. "Wait until you see them tonight."

"I'm sure no one in town misses seeing them." Libby grinned as she climbed into her car.

"Have a good day out, dear." Cyn waved her off.

Libby wasn't sure what she would do with her free day, but she knew she wasn't going to stay in the apartment. Instead, she headed for the mall on the edge of town.

The parking lot was already decorated with garlands and twinkling lights, and inside, children's voices were singing about Santa coming to town.

The holiday Libby had been dreading since Labor Day was almost here. It appeared no matter where Matthias sent her, she wouldn't be able to escape Christmas.

"Don't be a Scrooge, Libby," she muttered to herself as she noticed teenage elves keeping small children in line as they waited their turn to tell Santa what they wanted for Christmas.

It wasn't long before Libby felt herself fall into the holiday mood. Memories came back to her as she stood in front of one of the department stores.

She'd gotten Tyler's Christmas gift here last year—a woodworking saw he'd hungered for. She'd had Sara's picture taken professionally for special photos for family members. She'd also bought many gifts for their baby, even ones she wasn't old enough to enjoy.

Libby had purchased for her mother a gold chain with a little-girl charm holding Sara's birthstone, telling Marie she hoped there would be more birthstone charms to add to the chain. So her father wouldn't feel left out, she'd found a money clip that she could add Sara's birthstone to and had engraved on it Grampa's Little Darlings. Her mother had cried when she opened her present. Even her father had a few tears in his eyes when he held his money clip.

A rather, more painful memory suddenly materialized in Libby's mind.

The day had been too beautiful for a funeral. The sun shone brightly overhead. Flowers bloomed everywhere and were in evidence as a floral blanket on the tiny white coffin.

Libby had felt so numb that day she hadn't truly noticed her mother crying into a handkerchief. Her father had stood stiffly behind Marie's chair, his eyes damp with tears. Her sister and brothers appeared to be in shock, as if they couldn't believe the reason for their presence. And Tyler...he was the one who'd broken her heart. He stood beside her looking uncomfortable in his dark suit, his jaw tight with suppressed emotion and his eyes dark. He'd held on to Libby's hand with a grip that left bruises on her pale skin.

Why had it taken her this long to realize he had hurt as much as she did that day? How could she have ignored him the way she had?

She really had hidden herself away from everyone. She didn't want to have people pitying her for being unable to keep her baby alive. She didn't want to hear them talk in soft whispers about what a shame her loss had been. Or to listen as they told her she could have more children.

Now she realized Matthias had been right. She hadn't allowed herself to heal, to let the love of others help her to heal.

All right, Matthias, you made your point.

I never doubted you, my dear. You've made another large step. Be proud of yourself.

"Look who's here!"

Libby spun around at the sound of a familiar voice...and froze.

Marie Bennett was hurrying toward her, and she wasn't alone.

Oh Daddy! she cried inside, as she watched a gray-haired man walk toward her.

"Nathan, this is Libby Douglas. She's the teacher who's taking Bonnie's place at Miss Regina's," Marie told her husband after greeting Libby with a quick hug. "Libby, this is my better half, Nathan."

Libby forced a smile to her lips and took her father's outstretched hand.

"I'm very pleased to meet you, Mr. Bennett."

"Call me Nathan, please," he told her. "How are you liking our town so far?"

"I'm still getting used to all the changes," she said truthfully.

"I love it when everyone starts decorating for Christmas," Marie said to Libby. Her face was alight as she looked around the mall. "Starting next weekend, the high school chorus is out here every Sunday afternoon to sing. You should come and hear them.''

''I'll try.'' Libby attempted not to be too obvious as she studied her father.

Was he watching his diet? Taking the walks the doctor insisted upon? She used to goad her father into walking with her, but then she remembered the last time they'd walked together was with Sara in the stroller. Nathan Bennett loved to play the proud grandpa while everyone oohed and ahhed over the baby.

He looked a bit heavier than she remembered. And a little tired.

''We're off to get some shopping done,'' Marie told her. ''It was so good to see you again.'' She hugged Libby once more. ''Please give Cyn my best.''

''I will,'' she promised. She felt forlorn the moment the couple left her.

Any idea of shopping seemed unappealing now. All the people she wanted to buy for didn't know her anymore. Libby wandered around aimlessly until she reached the movie theater. She checked the times and discovered a comedy would be showing in fifteen minutes.

''Oh sure, let's just go to the show,'' she muttered, digging out her wallet and purchasing a ticket.

Chapter Thirteen

"I should be giving the truck a tune-up," Tyler grumbled, pulling into a parking space and shutting off the engine.

He'd woken up feeling grumpy and just plain out of sorts. He told himself he should have awakened with a smile. Dammit, he should have greeted the morning with Libby all soft and warm in his arms.

After a breakfast of blueberry Pop Tarts and coffee, he decided it would be a good idea to tune up his truck today. He'd left home with the intention of driving over to the auto-parts store to pick up what he needed.

Instead, he cruised by the mall and, without thinking about it, turned in. Now he was walking inside and idly looking around.

If he'd thought about it, he probably would have been the first to be surprised he was walking up to the movie theater and purchasing a ticket.

"Hi, Tyler," the woman in the ticket booth greeted him as he pushed his money through the slot. A look of surprise crossed her face. "What are you doing here?"

He shrugged. "Hi, Kate. I'm putting off tuning up my truck."

She chuckled and shook her head. "Sounds like my David. Except he has the kids to help him."

"Which means he probably won't get anything done." Tyler grinned as he entered the theater.

As he purchased a large Coke and popcorn, he noticed a lot of parents with their kids going in to see the latest Disney film.

Tyler had never thought of himself as a potential parent. He enjoyed other people's kids, but what he enjoyed most was being able to give them back to Mom and Dad. Now he wondered if maybe being a dad wouldn't be so bad. He could easily visualize a little girl with tawny blond curls or a boy with dark hair like his own.

As he entered the theater, the lights were starting to dim. The first thing he noticed was it wasn't very full. The second thing he noticed was Libby sitting by herself toward the back. He waited a few minutes just in case she was with someone else. When it seemed clear she wasn't, he quickly headed toward her.

"This seat taken?" He swiftly sank into it before she could answer.

Her head snapped around and she stared at him, as if he was the last person she had expected to see.

"Popcorn?" He held out his large bucket. His eyes dropped, seeing the small container in her lap. "Oh, I see you have your own." He settled in, resting his tub of popcorn on his knee.

"What are you doing?" she whispered fiercely.

He looked straight ahead, as if entranced by the previews of upcoming films. "I thought I'd take in a show. It's allowed, you know."

Libby's mouth opened and closed like a fish out of water. "There are plenty of other empty seats."

He didn't wince at her pointed comment.

"I always think it's more fun to watch a movie with someone I know," he whispered back. "This movie is supposed to be good, isn't it?"

Libby turned back to watch the screen. Just a hint of a smile teased her lips. "I'm sure you'll love it. Explosions, lots of guns, men loaded with testosterone, women scantily clad...."

Tyler grinned at her sarcasm. "What can I say? There're times when a man has to watch all those shoot-'em-up movies."

As the opening credits began, Tyler scrunched down in his seat.

The more he thought about it, the more he wondered if this was actually the movie he'd meant to see. He couldn't remember which movie he'd bought a ticket for. Still, with Libby sitting next to him, he wasn't going to complain. He dug into the popcorn bucket and threw a handful into his mouth.

It didn't take Tyler more than five minutes to realize this was not a movie he would have chosen to lay out good money for.

"This is a chick film!" he exclaimed in a low voice.

"Ssh!" Libby glared at him.

Tyler slunk down farther in his seat. He only hoped none of his friends walked in here. He'd never live it down! Still, the chance to sit with Libby was worth suffering through a movie of women bonding and plotting against men. Oh sure, they were talking about finding "Mr. Right" and having their careers at the same time, but hell, they made it sound as if it was a war or something.

"Stop it!" she hissed, poking her elbow in his side.

He glared back at her. "Stop what?"

She glared daggers at him. "Stop making your male, asinine comments. If you didn't think you'd enjoy the movie, why did you come in here?"

"Good question," he muttered.

Tyler decided he'd better be quiet before Libby did more than poke her elbow in his side. He fidgeted as he listened to a conversation on the screen. Were men really that thoughtless? Just wanting sex and not looking for anything even semipermanent? Damn, he felt as if what the guy on the screen was saying was the same thing he'd said to Libby just last night.

The sinking feeling in Tyler's stomach now increased to a plummet.

Why is he here? Libby's mind kept asking the question, but the answer never seemed to materialize.

She nibbled on her popcorn and sipped her Diet Coke and tried to ignore the man seated next to her. She told herself that any man could have sat there. She could pretend it wasn't Tyler.

Except her imagination seemed to have taken a vacation. There was no way she could ignore him. He was hunched down in the seat munching on his popcorn and occasionally drinking his Coke. His eyes were fastened on the screen, but she was positive he wouldn't remember one word spoken.

She was beginning to doubt she'd remember anything, either. Every once in a while, his arm would brush against hers or the scent of his soap tickled her nostrils. She had hoped to wallow in a film that promised a few laughs and plenty of tears, but now she was determined not to. The last thing she wanted to do was show any emotion in front of him.

Yet no matter how many times she reminded herself to pretend he was a stranger, it didn't work. No matter how many times she warned herself not to give in to the emotional theme of the film, it didn't work. She sniffed several times in hopes of keeping the tears back. Then she reared back when something white suddenly appeared in front of her face.

"Don't worry, it's clean," he whispered.

Since she didn't even have a tissue in her purse, she accepted the handkerchief and dabbed at her eyes.

When Tyler, whose own eyes were still focused on the film, reached over and laced his fingers through hers and settled her hand on his knee, she didn't resist. The touch was too familiar. Too heartbreaking.

When the closing credits ended and the lights came back on, Libby had already turned Tyler's handkerchief into a damp, crumpled ball.

"I'm sorry," she said, holding it up. "I'll wash it before I return it."

He looked faintly embarrassed. "That's okay. My mamma taught me to always carry a clean handkerchief. I'm glad I remembered that rule."

Libby smiled. This was the Tyler she could never resist.

"Thank you."

As she left the theater, she realized he was shortening his stride to match hers.

"I see you haven't lost your touch, Tyler," Kate teased when they passed the ticket window. "Go in alone, come out with a woman."

"No fair, Kate," he muttered, ducking his red face.

"It seems everyone knows you only too well, Tyler Barnes," Libby murmured with a smile.

"Yeah, well..." He slid his fingers through hers. "What do you have planned for the rest of the day?"

"Nothing in particular." She shrugged.

"Then how about hanging out with me?"

Libby looked up at him. "Hanging out with you? Are we back in high school?"

Tyler glanced around, as if fearing someone would overhear him. He ducked his head until his lips almost touched her ear.

"I'm sorry about last night, Lib," he murmured. "I acted like a crude idiot."

She twisted her face upward, and looked at him, feeling almost shy. "Crude?" she murmured.

His gaze was fixed on her lips, which she imagined must glisten from the buttered popcorn she'd eaten during the movie.

He nodded, still staring hungrily. "Am I forgiven?"

She hesitated for a moment. "All right, I'll hang out with you. As long as that time doesn't include a trip to the hardware store."

Tyler grinned and tightened his grip on her hand. "Now how did you guess that was one of my favorite pastimes?"

Libby felt as if she was with the Tyler she had known in high school, teasing, lighthearted and just plain fun.

He suggested she leave her car in the mall parking lot and come with him. Once ensconced in his pickup truck, he assured her there would be no trips to the hardware store, but there would be a quick stop at the auto-parts store.

"Don't tell me. You want to work on your truck," she teased.

He looked embarrassed. "Not today, of course."

"Of course," she said gravely, suppressing her smile.

He stopped at a red light and looked over at her. "Will you think the worst of me if I ask you to stop by my house?"

"It depends on the reason."

"I need to let my dog out."

Dog? She couldn't stop staring at him.

"Of course."

If Libby hadn't known the neighborhood, she wouldn't have recognized the house.

While Tyler's parents had kept their house painted pale green with dark green trim for as many years as she could remember, it was now painted an off-white with dark blue trim. None of the flowers his mother had planted along the porch were there, either.

Libby stared at the four-foot plastic Santa standing on the front porch and imagined it brightly lit after dark. She could see the strings of multicolored lights covering the roof and stretched along the front porch. At least that hadn't changed.

"I see you decorate for the holidays," she commented.

"Yeah, I like the holidays." He hopped out of his truck and walked around to her door. He helped her down, then ran around to the bed of the truck to pick up his purchases from the auto-parts store. "You ought to see this place at Halloween. It's one of the best haunted houses around."

She smiled at his transparent pride. "Ah, the screams of tortured souls, cobwebs everywhere, bloody body parts slung all over the place to swing against unsuspecting faces, skeletons reaching out to grab unwary visitors and invite them into their hell."

"Bloody body parts," he murmured, then brightened. "That sounds cool. I'll have to remember that for next year. So what about Christmas?''

Her smile dimmed. "I'm not very fond of Christmas." She carefully pulled away from his grasp.

"I can't imagine anyone not liking Christmas. Around here, everyone gets together to celebrate. There's house-decoration contests, kids' pageants, you name it." He steered her around to the back of the house. "Groups go caroling. Santa goes around on a fire truck every Thursday night."

"With his high school helpers dressed up in scanty costumes," she murmured, remembering the Christmas she had been so happy to have been chosen to be one of Santa's helpers. She had almost froze in the process, and it had taken gallons of hot chocolate and Tyler's arms around her to warm her up.

Tyler looked at her quizzically.

"Same thing where I came from," she explained.

As they walked around the side of the house, Libby looked up at the green-garbed elves hanging from the eaves.

"There are other people who aren't fond of Christmas," she said.

"Not in this town."

She had to smile at his emphatic reply.

"For some people, Christmas holds sad memories."

Tyler stopped and looked down at her. "Sad memories don't need to be forgotten. Just tucked away to make room for new, happier ones."

She swallowed. Was that what Tyler had done? Tucked Sara away in a part of his heart where she would be safe and he would have room for more?

"Just let me put this stuff in the garage." Tyler touched her arm before loping off to a side door which he opened and disappeared through.

Libby looked around the large yard. With winter here, the lawn furniture was out of sight and the trees and shrubs were bare of leaves.

"I shouldn't have come here," she whispered to herself.

Tyler apologized and seemed very sincere. Besides, you were curious to see his house.

It didn't take long for the light to click on inside her brain. She spun around so her back was to the garage.

"You somehow got him to go to that movie, didn't you? He wouldn't have gone there on his own."

He only needed a bit of a nudge.

"I'm sorry, I should have let you into the house," Tyler apologized, walking up to her. "You must be freezing."

"Not yet. Besides, it was nice to just look around." She followed him up the steps.

Tyler opened the door, led her through the laundry room and into the kitchen. Warm air seemed to swirl around them.

"Would you like some coffee?" he asked, heading for the coffeepot.

Libby smiled at his attempt to be the proper host. Then she remembered that Tyler's idea of coffee was to have it strong enough to float the entire U.S. Navy. She kept her smile in place.

"That sounds fine."

Libby sat at the table and watched Tyler move around the kitchen. In no time, coffee was dripping into the pot. He checked a cabinet, made a face and pulled open the dishwasher door. He stared at the contents, sighed and withdrew two mugs. He quickly scrubbed them out.

"Did you forget to run the dishwasher?" she teased lightly.

"I run it when I run out of dishes," he explained as he poured coffee into the mugs and handed one to her. He picked up a chair, swung it around so the back leaned against the table and sat down. He leaned his arms on the chair back while cradling his mug.

Libby cautiously sipped the hot liquid. She was right—it was so strong she was positive it could peel the skin off the roof of her mouth. She could feel it burning all the way down to her stomach.

Tyler didn't miss the look on her face.

"Sorry, I tend to make it a little too strong. Do you want some milk or sugar?"

She shook her head. "No, I'll be fine." She hoped.

Tyler didn't take his eyes off Libby as he sipped his coffee.

"You're so beautiful."

She blushed. "I think the coffee has affected your brain."

He shook his head. "No, I thought you were beautiful the first time I saw you. I know this sounds weird, but I look at you and feel as if I've known you all my life."

"Be careful, Tyler. I might think you have a romantic soul."

"Maybe with you I do." He took a deep breath. "I acted like a real jerk last night. You were right. What we had last night was something I'd never had before. I felt..." He paused, shaking his head in bewilderment as he searched for the right words. "Damn, I don't know what I felt. Maybe that's why I was scared." He put down his mug and thrust his fingers through his hair.

Libby's hands shook as she set down her own mug.

"In the past year, I've gone through a lot of

emotional pain," she whispered. "I didn't know what to think, either. But I knew I couldn't allow you to demean what we shared."

Tyler reached across the table and covered her hand with his. "I think I was supposed to meet up with you today, Lib," he told her. "That way I could apologize before I lost my nerve."

A hint of a smile curved her lips. "I guess your sitting through that movie was punishment enough."

He groaned. "I'm sorry, I'm a stupid male who couldn't understand half of what went on there."

Libby got up and walked around to his side of the table. Tyler spun around in his chair to face her as she stood in front of him. She combed her fingers through his hair, pushing the unruly waves from his forehead. He kept his eyes on her face as he lifted his hands to hers.

"Maybe it's magic in the air. Maybe it's a virus."

He grinned at her lighthearted comment. "I'll go with the magic." His eyes darkened with desire.

He stood up, sliding his hands along her waist to keep her close to him. He lowered his face to hers and brushed his lips against her mouth.

His kiss was tentative, asking for more. She raised her arms, looping them around his neck as his kiss deepened. Her lips parted, accepting his seeking tongue. Soft-voiced murmurs floated around them as they stood there in each other's arms. They were lost in their own world.

Libby hazily thought she should feel guilty that she wanted to make love to him again. He was her husband, yet he wasn't.

Forget the semantics, Libby. This is your Tyler. That is all that counts.

She jerked back at the sound of Matthias's voice inside her head.

Tyler looked confused at her sudden movement. "Is there something wrong?"

Libby stared at him for a long time. She didn't recognize the shirt he wore or the interior of the kitchen, but she recognized the desire-filled look in his eyes and the desire that made his body taut.

She placed her fingertips against his lips. "There's nothing wrong," she whispered. "Nothing at all."

Sensing what she was truly saying, he caught her up in his arms. She smiled and kept her arms around his neck.

"I, uh, I didn't make the bed this morning," he said haltingly, as he walked through the house. "And I'm not the best housekeeper."

Libby kept her eyes on his face. She wondered what he would say if she told him she adored his uncertainty.

"You're safe. I didn't bring my white gloves

with me to check for dust.'' She pressed her mouth against his throat and gently nipped the skin. "It's a good thing you didn't make the bed. We'd muss it up again, wouldn't we?''

His laughter was shaky at best as he walked into the bedroom.

"I have to say, Teach, you know just the right thing to say at just the right time.''

Chapter Fourteen

From her vantage point in his arms, Libby was able to have a good look around the room.

Miniblinds were open a fraction to let in the light. Tyler hadn't minced words. Clothing was scattered on the floor leading to the bathroom, a damp towel was slung into the sink and the chest of drawers was covered with an equal amount of dust and personal items.

Tyler let her down, sliding her down as slowly as possible against his aroused body.

"I want you so much," he whispered, his voice raw with need. "But I don't want to make any mistakes this time."

She was touched by his admission.

"Then just listen to your heart," she whispered back as she began unbuttoning his shirt.

They took their time undressing each other. They explored each other's bodies as thoroughly as could be done, pleased when either would find a sensitive spot.

Libby discovered this Tyler's arousal points were the same as her first Tyler's. The tender skin behind his ear. The curve of his shoulder. And behind his knee. Wherever her fingers or lips touched, he moaned her name.

They lay naked on the rumpled covers, content to caress each other.

Libby trailed her hands over Tyler's chest. Crisp brown hairs curled around her fingers as she found his nipples. She touched the coppery brown peaks with her tongue and smiled when he groaned and moved under her touch.

"You like that, do you?"

"Very much." He gulped in heavy breaths of air, then swiftly moved over her and circled his tongue around her nipple. "Turnabout's fair play."

But Tyler couldn't be content with that. He felt as if he needed to study every inch of Libby's body. He felt the need to crawl inside her and find out everything he could.

He'd never felt such strong, intense desire for a woman before. Yet all he had to do was look at Libby, experience her smile, and he wanted to take her away and keep her all to himself.

He tunneled his hands through her hair, feeling the silky softness against his skin. He buried his face in the silken mass, inhaling the scent that was all hers. When he placed his hand against her taut belly, for a brief moment he thought of her swollen with child and felt the pride of knowing the child was of their making.

His hand moved downward to the triangle of dark blond hair and farther down to find her moist and welcoming to his touch. He inserted one finger, then two, feeling her close around him. Libby arched up, crying out as he discovered the tiny nub of her pleasure.

"Libby?" He looked into her face, seeing passion cloud her eyes and tighten her features.

She smiled as she wrapped her hand around his erection and squeezed lightly. He groaned at the exquisite pain.

"Tyler Barnes, if you don't finish what you started I will make you very sorry," she murmured.

He wiggled his eyebrows. "Really? Are we talking kinky here?"

Libby was already lost. This was her Tyler. It had been so long since they'd indulged in teasing love play like this. And she knew exactly what to do.

"More like this." She encircled his erection with her hand and dipped her head downward.

From the first touch of Libby's lips on his ultrasensitive skin, Tyler felt as if the air had been punched out of his stomach.

"Libby." His voice was raw with need. He grasped her shoulders, pulling her upward to meet him. Their mouths fused at the same time Tyler rose up and thrust into Libby's waiting softness.

She cried out with joy and arched up to meet him.

"Look at me," he ordered. When her eyes still didn't open, he repeated his words. Her eyes swept open and stared back at him.

He could already feel his body wanting release. He threaded his fingers through hers, anchoring her hands onto the bed by her head.

"Together, Libby."

"Together," she whispered.

The word barely left her lips before they both shot upward into the heavens. Before they had a chance to come down, the explosion happened again.

Afterward, Tyler rolled onto his side and wrapped his arms around Libby, pulling her back against his chest.

"Now this is what I call perfect." He brushed her hair back with his fingers and dropped a kiss on her ear.

"Arrogant male."

"Because of you, darlin'. Because of you."

Libby curved her hands around his wrists, relishing the warmth of his skin against her palms. She lay there staring at the window, noticing the light starting to dim.

How many times have we lain just like this? she asked herself. *How many times did we make love with the thought of conceiving a child? But there was more to our marriage than children. We had each other, Tyler, and I abandoned you when you needed me most. Oh Tyler, how could I have done such a thing?* Tears ran unheeded down her cheeks and onto his wrist.

"Libby?" He raised up on one elbow so he could look down upon her face. "What's wrong?"

She clutched the arm still around her chest. The tears refused to cease and she could only shake her head.

Tyler had never liked tears. They usually frustrated him, since he felt as if women used tears to control him. Yet he instinctively knew Libby wasn't using her tears to manipulate. Something was truly making her sad.

He sat up and pulled her onto his lap, keeping his arms tightly around her as she buried her face against his chest and sobbed brokenly.

"Libby, please tell me what's hurting you," he begged.

"Let me make it better."

She shook her head, still unable to speak.

"Please?" He wiped her eyes with his fingers.

She took several deep breaths and soon her tears lessened.

"I had a baby girl," she whispered.

This wasn't something he'd expected to hear.

"Where is she?" He didn't want to think the baby's father had taken her child from her or something equally distressing.

"She died." Her voice was a bare rasp. She looked away. "Sara was only a few months old. She just didn't wake up one morning. They call it SIDS." Libby wiped her face with her hand. "I didn't want her to die. I didn't want to put her into the earth where she would be alone. So I allowed my grief to rule my life. I didn't want anyone to tell me things would get better."

He rested his cheek against the top of her head. "What about the father?" He didn't want to ask, but he had to know.

She was quiet for so long he didn't think she was going to answer him.

"He wanted to go on. He wanted us to have another baby. I couldn't do it." She kept staring at the window. "I was afraid."

"So he left you?" Tyler couldn't imagine any man wanting to leave Libby. He hadn't known her for long, but he felt as if he'd known her forever.

She pulled herself free from his embrace and slid off the bed.

"Libby?"

She didn't stop on her way to the bathroom until she reached the doorway. She kept her back to him as she whispered, "I left him."

LIBBY WAS GRATEFUL she could find a clean towel in the bathroom, so she wouldn't have to go back out and ask for one.

She turned on the shower. Luckily, the temperature was easily adjusted and she could step into the stall. Under the stream of hot water she could cry without being overheard.

I'm proud of you, Libby. You were able to speak out about Sara.

"I don't want anyone feeling proud of me." She wiped her hands over her face. "Talking about Sara didn't feel good at all. I hurt all over."

With her face upturned to the spray of water, she didn't hear the shower door open and Tyler step in.

She cried out when she was turned around and enfolded in a pair of arms. When she tried to struggle free, the embrace only tightened. She buried her face against his shoulder and tried to stifle her sobs.

"It's okay to cry," he murmured in her ear, running his hands up and down her back in a soothing caress.

"I was a horrible mother!" she sobbed, gripping his shoulders.

"I don't know a lot about babies, but I have heard about SIDS, and no one knows why it happens." He kept his lips close to her ear. "It's not your fault, Libby. Did your husband blame you for what happened?"

She shook her head.

"Did he accuse you of neglect?"

Again she shook her head.

"Did he want your marriage to end?"

There was a pause before she shook her head.

"Then let go of all that hurt, Libby." He kept rubbing her back.

"I can't!" she sobbed.

"Yes, you can." He reached past her and switched off the water. He pushed the door open and grabbed a towel, which he wrapped around her. He plopped a second towel on top of her head and began rubbing vigorously until Libby protested.

"I won't have any hair left," she said, holding up her hands.

His touch immediately gentled.

Libby stepped out of the shower, wrapping the towel around her and tucking a corner in to keep it secure. She leaned over the sink to get a better look in the mirror. She mumbled something incoherent and slicked her wet hair back.

"You don't look that bad," Tyler protested, taking another towel from a cabinet and wrapping it around his waist.

"I'm not fishing for compliments," she said, picking up a tissue and wiping away specks of smeared mascara from under her eyes.

"Libby, you didn't do anything wrong. It seems you were so busy not forgiving yourself for something you couldn't control that you decided to punish yourself," he said quietly. "Don't you think you've been too hard on yourself? That's why you moved away from Webster Falls, isn't it? Because it happened there?"

Her laughter held no humor. "Oh, I ran much farther away than that. You have no idea how far."

He walked over and settled his hands on her shoulders. As if sensing she didn't want comfort, he waited a moment before speaking.

"Don't let this get around, but I'm a real jerk," he stated.

Libby's eyes snapped upward.

He turned her around and placed his forefinger against her lips.

"Now, now, I don't want to hear what a charmer I am and such a perfect gentleman. I've been a jerk because we've made love two days in a row and I haven't even taken you out on a date.'' There was a look of pained embarrassment in his eyes.

Libby reared her head back. "I guess I'll just have to agree with you."

"Then how about dinner out tonight?"

"I'll need to go home and freshen up. But first you'll have to drive me back to my car."

"Done." He wasn't taking any chances. He pulled a hair dryer out of the cabinet and handed it to her. "I'll go get dressed." He walked out, closing the door after him.

Libby collapsed against the counter.

"Matthias." She hissed the name. "Dammit, where are you?"

I'm right here. His deep sigh was evident. *You should feel much better now after coming out and telling him what happened.*

"Then why aren't I back where I belong?"

It's not that easy.

"I already figured that out." She plugged in the hair dryer and turned it on. "I hate you."

I never said it would be easy.

Libby dried her hair in record time, then ventured out into the bedroom. She found her clothes neatly laid on the bed and quickly put them on.

After she dressed, she found Tyler in the living room. He stood at the front window looking out. As if he sensed her presence, he turned around.

"Ready to go?"

She nodded.

As they walked outside, Libby was aware of Tyler's arm around her shoulders.

"Miss Libby! Miss Libby!"

She stopped from climbing into Tyler's truck and turned toward the street. A familiar red-haired child ran toward her.

"Becca? Do you live around here?" She crouched down to the little girl's level.

Her head bobbed up and down. "Me and Mrs. Robinson and King Tut live over there." She pointed two houses up the street. Her eyes shifted from Libby to Tyler. "Is he your boyfriend?" she asked in a loud whisper.

Libby felt her cheeks burning.

"I'd like to think I am." Tyler spoke for Libby. "So your name's Becca? You must be in Miss Libby's class at Miss Regina's."

Becca stared up at him. "You'll be a very good daddy."

"Well, thank you, darlin'." He flashed her a grin. "Although I may not find that out for a while."

Becca looked back at Libby. "And you'll be a good mommy. I want a mommy just like you," she said in her whispery voice.

Libby's smile seemed to freeze on her face as she stared at the girl. She slowly reached out and touched Becca's cheek with the back of her fingers.

"What do you know, Becca?" she whispered.

Becca's smile didn't hold any of the wistfulness it had before.

"You know, Miss Libby. You really do." She bobbed forward, kissed her on the cheek and ran off.

Libby slowly straightened up. She couldn't keep her eyes off the small figure skipping along the sidewalk.

"Cute kid," Tyler commented, not noticing the intensity of Libby's gaze. "I bet you looked just like her when you were her age."

"I guess I did," she murmured.

Libby was aware of Tyler's questioning looks as he drove her back to her car. She wasn't sure what to say to him. She knew she couldn't tell him the truth.

"Are you all right?" he asked her as he waited by her car while she unlocked the door.

She started to nod, then saw the look of uncertainty on his face.

"It's not you," she assured him, touching his arm.

"Don't feel bad about the little girl saying you'd be a good mom." He apparently misunderstood. "A good teacher like you is bound to be a good mom."

She shook her head, amused by his comment. "You've never seen me teach."

He dipped his head and nuzzled her ear. "Hey, you can keep me after school anytime. I'll pick you up at seven, okay?"

She shivered under the warmth of his breath. "I'll be ready."

"So will I." There was no doubt what he was talking about. "You better get in your car before I change my mind and order in pizza."

"Oh no, we are definitely going out." She slid into her car and started the engine. Tyler stood nearby until she drove off.

"Well, well, look who's teacher's pet."

Tyler mouthed a pithy curse before he turned around to face the speaker.

"Hello, Renee," he said calmly.

"Hello my butt," she snarled. "I won't even ask you what you were doing with her. That was pretty obvious! What I want to know is why with *her?*" Renee had one hand on her hip as she glared at him.

Tyler studied the woman standing before him and couldn't help comparing her to the woman who'd just left.

Renee's hair was brushed in a casual style that intimated she'd just gotten out of bed. Her makeup was too artfully applied, from her gray eye shadow and navy liner to her red-glossed lips.

Her sweater looked to be one size too small in order to show off her full breasts, and her jeans were also more than a little too tight. She wore her coat open so no man would miss her.

Tyler felt as if a light had gone on inside him. He had lusted after Renee for years, and yes, he'd finally gotten her. But he had always felt as if he needed more. Now he knew. Renee had always seen him as a trophy she could display to everyone. As if she'd won some contest.

Libby had given him a hard time, yes, but he deserved it. And he doubted she'd ever view him as a prize. Now he wished he could give her everything she deserved. And she deserved a hell of a lot more than he could ever give her.

Renee's eyes were flat with hate as she stared at him.

"So the teacher is nothing more than a little slut. I wonder what the sainted Miss Regina would think about that," she taunted.

Tyler didn't hesitate. He strode toward her until he stood over her.

"You will not say anything negative about Libby, do you hear me?" He spoke low and furiously. "She's never done anything to you."

Renee wasn't about to back down. "She took you from me."

"Let me make this perfectly clear, Renee. I was never yours to begin with," he stated in a tone that brooked no argument. "We had a lot of laughs. I'm sorry it ended this way between us."

Her furious expression took any beauty out of her face.

"If you want someone like her, then you aren't the man I thought you were, Tyler. Just don't come crawling back to me when she decides she wants a man who has some class." She turned on her heel and walked swiftly away.

Tyler watched her hips wiggling from side to side as she approached the mall entrance.

"You never lose your touch, Renee," he murmured before he headed back to his truck. "And I'm sure in no time you'll find someone to console you."

Chapter Fifteen

"It's just a dinner date," Libby kept repeating, as if it was an important chant. The words were meant to calm her, but they did the exact opposite.

She took another shower and afterward rubbed a body lotion all over her body, which not only left a pleasant scent but shimmered under the light. She used a heavier hand than usual with her makeup as she shadowed her eyes with taupe and applied a dusty green liner. Tawny peach blush and lipstick were the finishing touches.

When she had stepped out of the shower, she had hot rollers on the counter all ready to go.

"I gather you approve of my going out this evening," she said out loud as she rolled her hair.

Yes, I do.

Libby narrowed her eyes. "You're not in this room, are you?"

Of course not. I would not dream of intruding upon a lady's toilette.

Libby fastened the last roller and dropped her arms.

"Becca has something to do with this, doesn't she?"

Is that what you think?

"I don't appreciate your answering me with another question." Libby fluffed her bangs with her fingers.

Then why are you asking me if I would use a small child to achieve my goal? I have trouble imagining you would even consider such a thought.

"Very funny." She starting taking out the rollers. Then she brushed her hair into a fluffy golden cloud swirling around her face.

You look very lovely, my dear.

Libby looked around with narrowed eyes. "I thought you couldn't see me."

Only when I wish, but I would never intrude when you require privacy.

"You better not."

She went into her bedroom and put on a calf-length wool skirt the shade of dark cinnamon and teamed it with a deep gold, hip-length sweater and brown boots.

"All right, Matthias, I admit you have excellent taste."

"Of course I do." He appeared at her side with a large, amber, oval-shaped pendant, which he handed to her. A pair of matching earrings were next. "Someone had to do something. A scullery maid couldn't have dressed as drably as you were."

"I should be offended, but I'm not." Libby added the jewelry and stepped back to admire the entire effect. "Not as flashy as Renee, but I'll do."

"Tyler has never truly cared for Renee as he has come to care for you, Libby," he told her. "From the beginning, he sensed there was something special about you. I am sure you can see that the two of you were always meant to be together."

"I wasn't sure at first. He was so different from the Tyler I knew."

"That was because you were not here. He grew up more a rebel until he started settling down a few years ago. Now he's starting to realize it's time to settle down even more."

Libby felt an uneasy feeling settling in her stomach.

"I can't stay here, Matthias. He's Tyler, yes, but he's not the Tyler I fell in love with."

"He is your Tyler. He is just a Tyler you met later in life."

A staccato tap at the door startled her. She knew it had to be Tyler.

"Have a good evening, Libby." Matthias was gone in a blink of the eye.

Libby picked up her coat and purse and headed for the door. When she opened it, she was surprised to find Tyler wearing a crisply ironed blue shirt and a neatly knotted tie under his brown leather jacket.

"You look beautiful," he said softly.

"Tyler, you look as if you're strangling in that tie." She tried not to smile at his apparent discomfort, but her lips still tilted upward. "Does the restaurant we're going to require a tie?"

He shook his head. "I just wanted to show you I can be a gentleman."

"And you've done it beautifully. Now please take it off before you choke."

He breathed a sigh of relief as he tugged the knot loose, then pulled the tie off over his head. As Tyler tucked it into his jacket pocket, Libby reached up and unfastened the top shirt button. She smoothed his collar down and gave it a gentle pat.

"Now your face isn't turning purple," she teased.

He had the grace to look sheepish. "I guess you can tell I don't wear ties too much."

"No reason when you don't need to."

Tyler took her coat and helped her into it. His hands rested on her shoulders.

"If I want to get you to that restaurant, I better keep my hands off," he murmured, guiding her outside.

They had just reached Tyler's truck when Cyn walked out the back door.

"Tyler Barnes—my, don't you look handsome tonight." She walked over, a vision in fuchsia and cobalt blue under a purple wool cape that swept down to her ankles. She turned to study Libby. "I must say, the two of you make a handsome couple." Her eyes gleamed with delight. "Lovey, this man is known for his conquests. Make sure you break his heart before he breaks yours."

"Cyn, you are a wicked woman," Tyler teased, dropping a kiss on her cheek. "And," he said in a mock whisper, "the lady already has my heart."

"Have a good evening, children." She stared Tyler down. "And no hanky-panky this time."

Libby gulped. Cyn did know about his staying over that night.

Her landlady headed for the garage. "The Bennetts are coming over to play bridge," she announced. "I hope I have another bottle of Bordeaux out here. Have a good time."

Libby frowned. Her parents didn't play bridge. They hated bridge! But then, Tyler's parents were living in Arizona, so she had to accustom herself to all these changes.

"I just bet I know who the fourth in that bridge game is," Tyler said slyly.

Libby grinned. "So do I. I don't think the poor man has a chance."

The restaurant Tyler chose was on the edge of town and made up to look like an old English manor house. The place was familiar to her even though she'd never been inside. Dinner here was a treat she and Tyler had planned to give themselves when Sara was older. Libby felt a twinge of guilt that she would be experiencing it now.

They were seated in one of the dining rooms near a fireplace that roared merrily. The way the tables were situated, each was given a certain degree of privacy.

"This is lovely." Libby smiled at the maître d' as he handed her a menu.

"I've never been here before, but I thought you would like it," Tyler murmured.

She felt warmth deep down at the knowledge he'd never brought another woman here.

Tyler accepted the waiter's suggestion for wine and they chose their meals.

All through dinner, Libby kept Tyler talking about the town and its residents, under the guise of learning more about her new home. She heard familiar names, and by getting him to talk about his high school experiences was able to reconcile his memories with her own.

"It's not fair you've had me talking all evening," he complained as they were served a lemon soufflé for dessert. "I want to find out about you."

"You already know everything about me. When I arrived here, I was starting a new life," she told him as she tasted the soufflé and enjoyed the tart tang of lemon in her mouth.

Tyler's eyes darkened as he reached across the table and took her hand in his.

"I'd like to think I'm part of that new life," he said huskily.

Libby could feel the heat settling low in her center and fanning outward. By the slight widening of his eyes, she knew Tyler felt the same way.

He coughed a couple of times to clear his throat.

"Check, please."

ONCE THEY WERE SETTLED in the truck with the heater going, Tyler's first thought was to go back to his house or Libby's apartment. But dammit! He wasn't going to. He already knew Libby was someone very special. He could feel it in his bones. The last thing he wanted was to screw this up. He cast about his mind for something to do. As he drove past a brightly lit corner, he discovered just the thing.

"Let's get you a tree," he said suddenly.

Libby's head snapped around. "Excuse me?"

"A tree." He pulled over to the curb and parked the truck. "It's Christmas. You need a tree."

She looked uneasy as he helped her out of the truck. "I don't need a tree."

"Everyone needs a tree." He grabbed her hand and pulled her down to the tree lot. Christmas music blared out from loudspeakers and a large inflated Santa stood on top of the tent, his mittened hand waving back and forth.

Tyler ignored Libby's pathetic attempt to dig in her heels.

"I'll get my tree, too. Will that make you feel better?"

"Not really," she said, pulling back with no avail.

By now they were onto the lot.

Libby took a deep breath. "I admit the fresh smell of pine is great." She tentatively touched a branch of evergreen.

"Here you go." Tyler pulled out one tree and held it for her inspection.

Her eyes grew to the size of saucers. "It's got to be twelve feet tall!"

He tipped his head back. "Damn! You're right. We could cut a hole in your roof."

"We could not!"

"Okay, we can cut the top off."

"What's wrong with it going in your house?"

"Are you kidding? It's way too tall." He put the tree back.

Tyler led her over to another section of the lot where the trees were shorter. He chose a variety and held them out for Libby's inspection. She entered into the spirit by seriously considering each one's good and bad points.

"It's too short."

"Too tall."

"Too full."

"Too skinny."

"That one side is way too thin."

"It's crooked."

"The top is cut all wrong so you can't put a star or angel on it."

Tyler held what must have been the tenth tree while Libby circled it, stopping to check a branch or roll the needles between her fingers to ensure they weren't too dry.

"It just doesn't look right," she said finally.

"What do you mean it doesn't look right? The top is fine, the needles aren't dry and it's not the least bit crooked." Tyler advanced on her until they were toe-to-toe. "Libby Douglas, you will take this tree or I will kiss you senseless in front of every person here," he whispered.

Devilish lights seemed to sparkle in her eyes

while she hesitated, as if wondering whether he would actually follow through with his threat. Or if she would mind if he did. "It's a lovely tree."

"Damn straight."

"Now we have to find yours."

Tyler looked around, grabbed a tree, shook it out and looked it up and down. "Perfect."

If Libby thought differently she didn't say anything. A drop of something cold landed on her nose. She looked up and cried out with delight.

"It's starting to snow!"

"Hey, Tyler, you two finally pick out a tree?" one of the men in the tent called out. Laughter followed his question.

Tyler looked at Libby's face as more questions were directed their way, some a bit ribald. Her nose was pink from the cold, but he sensed the pink dotting her cheeks wasn't from the biting air.

"I know. They can't help themselves," she guessed. "They see a pretty girl and remember their own randy days."

He was taken aback by her statement. "You read minds?"

She shook her head. "Just human nature."

He brushed the back of his fingers against her cheek. "I'll take care of the trees. You get back in the truck to stay warm." He handed her the keys, his fingers lingering as they touched Libby's.

She nodded and walked swiftly away. Tyler was vastly grateful for the cold air that dampened his arousal so quickly. The men in the tent would have had a field day with him.

He paid for the trees and had them loaded in the truck bed in no time. The motor was already running and the truck interior warm.

Libby gave him a sly smile. "So did they offer you their age-old advice on how to handle a woman?"

He grimaced. "I guess you could say that." He shifted gears.

Libby sat by him, their thighs touching.

"I didn't want to celebrate this Christmas," she said suddenly.

Tyler didn't have to ask what she meant. He merely took her hand in his and laid it on his right thigh. No words were spoken because none were needed.

"LOOK AT CYN'S HOUSE!"

Libby laughed as Tyler drove into the driveway of the house, which was dripping with colored lights. Candy canes lined the walkway to the front porch and the perimeter of the yard. Two wooden soldiers stood guard at the end of the driveway, while a lighted snowman stood in the middle of the yard.

"She said she always did it up big," Libby said. "I just had no idea she went this far."

"Look up at the roof," Tyler suggested.

She craned her neck and could see Santa in his sleigh with his reindeer perched on the roof.

"What do you think, Teach? A little over-done?"

She could only shake her head. She was afraid if she opened her mouth she'd start laughing and not be able to stop.

Tyler carried Libby's tree into her apartment and set it in a corner of the living room.

"I guess I'll be buying decorations for a tree." Libby stood back to make sure it was straight in its stand.

Tyler came up behind her and wrapped his arms around her body.

"While I'd like nothing more than to stay, I'm going to be a gentleman and say good-night." He turned her in his arms and brushed his lips against hers, then deepened their kiss. By the time he lifted his head, she was clinging to him. He took a deep breath to still the forest fire raging inside him. With great reluctance, he stepped back. "Good night, Libby." His voice was husky with desire.

"Good night, Tyler." She followed him to the door.

"Libby? Tyler?" Cyn stood in her back door.

"Why don't you two come over for some cake and coffee?"

"Sorry, Cyn, I have to get up early and try my miserable best to outdo you with decorations this year," Tyler called back as he walked to his truck.

"What about you, Libby?"

She was sorely tempted to see her parents again, but she wasn't sure she could handle the pain of acting as if they were virtual strangers.

"I'm sorry, Cyn, but I'm pretty tired. Perhaps another time?" she called back.

"I'll hold both of you to that."

Cyn noticed Tyler still hadn't gotten in his truck. She smiled at him and disappeared back into her house.

Tyler looked up at Libby and blew her a kiss. "Can I call you tomorrow?"

She grinned as she thought back to their dating days and some of their ridiculous jokes. "I'd rather you call me Libby, but it's up to you."

He groaned. "And to think you're a teacher."

Libby stood outside until Tyler backed down the driveway. Then she went inside, pulled off her coat and draped it over the back of a chair.

She curled up on the couch and thought about her evening with Tyler. It had been fun. How many times had her husband suggested they go out for the evening? And how many times had she refused because she didn't want to see anyone she knew? She'd shut herself up in the house because, in her mind, it was easier. She feared she would see people who would either accuse her of neglecting Sara or would comfort her when she didn't want to give herself comfort. She sighed.

"Poor Tyler. How did you put up with me during that time?"

She pushed herself off the couch with the intention of changing into a nightgown and watching television. Before she did either, she took a peek out the front window in hopes of seeing either of the Bennetts. But the curtains were closed.

Libby was alone again.

Chapter Sixteen

Libby found herself having breakfast by her Christmas tree, now decorated with shiny balls, little angels, twinkling lights and iridescent tinsel.

She might have thought about shopping for tree decorations the day before, but Tyler had had another idea. He'd showed up with bags of decorations. While unpacking them, he'd requested a cup of coffee and suggested she warm up the muffins he'd brought with him.

Libby knew it had been some time since she had enjoyed decorating so much. After they finished, Tyler kissed her on the forehead and reminded her it was a school night so she should get a good night's sleep. She was reluctant to see him go, but knew it was best.

When she arrived at the school, she found some of the workmen, including Tyler, carrying small trees into the building.

"Gee, haven't we done this before?" he whispered, winking at her as he carried a tree into her room. "You look like an elf," he murmured on the way out, referring to the festive red-and-green sweater and matching skirt Matthias had whipped up for her that morning.

"What shall we do with our tree?" she asked the class as they stood around it. Tyler had placed it on a small table.

"Put glitter on it!"

"Can we spray paint it?"

"Make decorations!"

"Will Santa leave presents under this tree, too?"

"Will my presents be under this tree or my tree at home?"

Libby took a deep breath.

"We'll put a special glitter on it. No, we can't spray paint it. We will make decorations. Santa might leave something special under this tree, but you'll find all your presents under your trees at home."

"Wow." Josh looked suitably impressed with her answering all the questions in order. "Can we make any kind of decoration we want?"

"As long as it looks like a Christmas decoration." She knew him well enough to know she had to give him a specific answer or he would probably come up with something that worked better for Halloween.

Libby had them sit at their tables and started some of them making colorful paper chains, while others were folding up pieces of white paper and cutting them out in the shapes of snowmen, angels and snowflakes. She walked around, assisting where necessary and admiring a finished product. She made sure her walk ended with Becca.

The little girl was slowly but carefully cutting into folds of white paper.

Libby looked at the one finished item.

"Becca, this is very good," she exclaimed, picking up the shape of an angel.

She looked up and smiled. "Can I put gold glitter on her wings?"

"Of course." Libby sat in a tiny chair by her. "Becca?"

The girl looked up from her task. "I wish I could have shown you King Tut Saturday, but he was mad at me again and he hid under Mrs. Robinson's bed."

"I'm sure you will have a chance to show him to me some other time." She lowered her voice. "Becca, you talked to me about my being a mother."

Becca's gaze was solemn as she stared at her teacher. "Sometimes kids can't have parents because their parents don't want them," she explained. "You should be a mommy, Miss Libby. Make a little girl happy."

Libby felt a chill all the way down to her bones. She started to touch Becca's cheek, but held back at the last minute. The girl continued watching her with eyes that now seemed very very old.

"Becca's a good name, isn't it?" the girl asked.

Libby nodded, because she couldn't say a word.

"Children! I have a wonderful announcement to make." Miss Regina entered the room with a bright smile on her face. "Miss Bonnie had a baby boy early this morning."

All the children jumped up and down and cheered.

"She was real smart to have a boy instead of some dumb girl," Josh said.

"Well, it looks like we'll have to make something special for Miss Bonnie, doesn't it?" Libby announced. "Let's finish the decorations we're working on now, then we'll make a very special card for her and her baby."

The entire class cheered and ran back to their chairs to finish up their projects.

Libby laid a large piece of white cardboard on the floor and urged each child to decorate part of it in his or her own way. The theme, loosely, was babies and things babies liked to do. She sat on the floor helping when asked and making suggestions. Along with that, she also asked each child what could be done to help take care of a baby. She was surprised by some of their answers since many children already proved to be well informed on the subject.

She sighed when she stopped to study Josh's section.

"Josh, are you drawing what I think you're drawing?"

He looked up. He knelt on the floor, where he had a corner of the cardboard to himself.

"I'm just showin' what babies do," he protested, pointing to the drawing he'd started in pencil. "And you gotta admit they do it a lot. Do we have any more brown crayons?"

"You cannot show that on the card," she told him firmly. "Draw something else babies do. Playing in a playpen or crawling on the floor or something."

Josh looked puzzled for a few minutes as he thought about Libby's suggestions. He suddenly brightened and leaned over to erase his drawing. Libby heaved a sigh of relief and moved on to one of the other children.

It took them two hours to decorate the large poster board the way they wanted, but they were all happy with it.

"A baby playing?" Libby pointed to Josh's section where a baby wearing a black-and-white-striped playsuit was in a playpen that looked more like a prison cell.

He nodded. "Cool, huh?"

Libby couldn't help but laugh. "Oh Josh, you are definitely one of a kind." She picked up the poster board and set it out of the way so it wouldn't be damaged. At the same time she instructed the children to put away the crayons. "I'll take this over to Miss Bonnie tonight. I know she'll love what you made for her."

"Can we finish making stuff for the tree?" Blake asked.

"After lunch we will."

Libby found herself watching Becca more and more as the day progressed. She puzzled over her words and could only come up with one conclusion. Except it was too incredible for her to believe.

The snow from the weekend left a thin white blanket on the ground, so the children played games indoors. Libby sat on a bench watching them play Simon Says. As always, Becca stood at the back of the line, the last to play. As if she sensed Libby studying her, she turned and smiled. Her smile was filled with reassurance. She walked over to Libby and patted her hand.

"Everything will be all right, Miss Libby," she said in her whispery voice.

Libby couldn't take her eyes from her.

"You look the way Sara would have at this age," Libby said in a barely audible voice.

"But I'm Becca," she corrected.

Libby nodded as if she understood. She thought she did, but she was afraid to voice what she thought.

By the time the day was over, she felt as if she had been working nonstop for weeks, not just eight hours. She smiled and said goodbye to the children as each was picked up. Becca was one of the last.

"Goodbye, Miss Libby." The little girl touched her hand.

She managed to smile. "Goodbye, Becca."

"You look exhausted," Miss Regina said as she entered the room.

Libby laughed. "I think I'm well past that stage. But the kids did so well today that it was worth all the energy I used up."

Miss Regina walked over to the poster-board card and studied it carefully.

"How did I know Josh would put a baby in a prison cell?"

"You should have seen what he first had the baby doing." Libby went on to explain.

Miss Regina helped her straighten up chairs against the tables.

"I thought I'd take the children's card over to the hospital tonight," Libby said.

"She'd appreciate that." Miss Regina patted her shoulder. "She's in room 310."

Libby nodded as she pulled on her coat, then picked up the large card.

"Good night, Miss Regina."

"Good night, dear."

When Libby walked outside, she found Tyler's pickup parked next to her car. He was leaning against her door and he cocked an eyebrow in question at the poster board she carried.

"Homework?"

"It's a baby card for Bonnie. I'm taking it to her."

"Care if I come along? We could get some dinner afterward," he suggested.

"All right, but we'll have to take my car so the card won't get ruined." She deactivated the door lock.

Tyler didn't hesitate climbing into the passenger seat.

"Do you need directions to the hospital?" he asked after she'd settled in and started up the engine.

"Yes, that would be helpful." She knew exactly where it was, but she feigned ignorance.

"This has to make Bonnie and Gary happy," Tyler commented, once they were on the road. "They've wanted a baby for a long time."

Libby nodded, because at the moment it was difficult to speak.

Tyler kept up light chatter throughout the drive. He talked about the work on the preschool building and what he heard Miss Regina had planned.

Eventually, Libby parked in the hospital parking lot and just sat there for a moment.

Tyler picked up one of her hands and found it cold to the touch.

"You should have worn gloves." He rubbed it briskly between his own and blew on the skin. He picked up her other hand and repeated the process. After he was done, held both hands between his and studied her set features. "You're nervous about going in, aren't you?"

She took a deep breath and nodded. "But I'm going to do it."

"Do you mind if I go in with you?"

"If you behave yourself," she advised.

"No scratching myself in improper places. No making animal noises to the baby." He shrugged. "Okay, but you're ruining all my fun."

She arched an eyebrow. "Come on, baby ape. Just be good."

Tyler carried the poster board in one hand and firmly grasped Libby's with the other. She found his silent support comforting as they walked into the hospital.

Libby made a quick stop in the gift shop to pick

up a floral arrangement, then felt a sinking sensation in the pit of her stomach as they crossed the lobby toward the elevators.

"Third floor," she said quietly when Tyler's fingers hovered over the control panel in silent query.

He kept hold of her hand as they stepped off the elevator. "So even if the baby looks like a little monkey I should still tell them he's cute?"

"Yes, you should." She squeezed his hand back, knowing he was just trying to ease her anxieties. "I'm all right, Tyler."

"Never thought you weren't." He pulled her close and kissed her thoroughly. Libby's eyes were glazed when he finished. "Okay, now you can go in."

She stumbled into the room with Tyler right behind her. Gary was seated on the side of the bed staring at the blanketed bundle in Bonnie's arms. The couple looked up, then looked again when they noticed Libby's escort.

"Congratulations, Gary." Tyler held out his hand. He peeked past the blanket. "Thank God the kid looks like Bonnie instead of you. He'll have a chance of getting a girl when the time comes."

"As if any kid with your ugly puss would have a chance," Gary retorted.

"Maybe if we ignore them they'll go outside

and do whatever men do to show who's tougher,'' Bonnie told Libby.

"Such as chew nails. This is from me." Libby set the floral arrangement on the table, then had Tyler hold up the card. "And this is from the class."

"How sweet." Bonnie's eyes glistened with tears. "I can't believe how crazy my hormones have been."

"New mothers are supposed to cry." Libby handed her a tissue.

Bonnie studied the card more fully. "I didn't even have to see Josh's name to know which drawing was his. I can't imagine this was his first choice."

Libby rolled her eyes. "I made the mistake of telling them to draw babies and what they do. Josh's excuse for what he started to draw was that babies did it a lot. I suggested something a little less graphic."

Gary leaned over, looked at the card and laughed.

"I'm sure glad we had a boy, honey," he told his wife. "I'd hate to think we could end up with Josh as a son-in-law."

Libby leaned over and gently folded back a corner of the blue blanket swaddling the baby. Her breath caught as she looked down at a tiny scrunched-up face with closed eyes and a rosebud mouth.

"I kept counting all his fingers and toes," Bonnie confessed, looking down with a tender smile. "I couldn't believe we were so lucky."

Libby smiled even though she felt like crying. "I guess all new mothers say that," she said huskily, keeping her trembling hands behind her back. She started when a warm hand grasped hers.

"I never thought a baby could be that small," Tyler commented. He wrapped a protective arm around Libby and grinned at Bonnie and Gary's silent exchange of questions. "Hey, I may be a little dense at times, but I know a good thing when I see it. I wasn't going to waste any time, either. Some guy who doesn't deserve her might have gotten there first." He dropped a kiss on top of Libby's head. "We hate to admire and run, but you've probably had people in and out all day and more to come tonight. Plus Libby gets cranky if she isn't fed every few hours."

Bonnie looked amused at Libby's expression of outrage.

"Thank you for coming. And for the flowers and card."

Libby leaned over and hugged Bonnie briefly. "I'm so glad for you." She thanked heaven that her voice didn't crack.

By the time they left the room, she felt ready to break down.

"You're doing fine, sweetheart," Tyler murmured, taking her arm as they stood in front of the elevators.

She gulped. "I knew it would be hard. I just didn't think it would be this hard," she whispered.

"Come on, let's get some food in you. I'll tell you some terrible jokes. You might not feel better, but you won't feel worse, either."

She laughed shakily at his teasing reassurance. "Oh, Tyler, if you only knew."

He swung her around as they exited the elevator. "Knew what?"

She stepped up to him and framed his face with her hands.

"If you only knew just how special you are," she said before kissing him.

The heat sparking between them would have increased in intensity if they hadn't been conscious of standing in a hospital lobby. They reluctantly parted and started toward the exit doors, but Tyler kept hold of one of her hands.

Libby skidded to a halt when Marie Bennett and her two sons came rushing into the hospital.

"Marie?" Libby reached out to stop her.

"Oh, Libby, hello." Her smile was vacant, her eyes red from weeping.

"Is something wrong?"

Marie's voice trembled. "My husband had a heart attack this afternoon."

Libby felt shock roll through her.

"I don't know how many times the doctor told him he had to watch his diet and get some exercise," Marie said with tears rolling down her cheeks. "But he never listened." She tried to smile and patted Libby's arm. She smiled at Tyler.

"Remind Nathan he won't want to lose his place at the poker games down at the VFW," Tyler told her. "You know how much he loves those poker games."

"I will."

Libby turned around and watched Marie and the two men head for the elevators.

You forgot me! she cried silently, still watching them. She yearned to run after them, to rejoin her family. *I need to see Daddy. Remember, Mom? How I'd nag him to watch what he ate and how we'd go for walks? Daddy has to get well!*

"Libby?" Tyler squeezed her hand. "You look so pale—are you all right?"

She squeezed back. "I hate to think of anyone sick."

"Food. You definitely need food." He wrapped an arm around her shoulders.

Libby wasn't certain she could eat a bite, but

with Tyler hovering about, she wasn't going to admit it.

She should have known he'd surprise her. He stopped at a Chinese restaurant, ordered takeout and propelled her back to her car.

"We are going to have our feast at your place," he informed her as he drove off. "I'll ply you with sweet-and-sour duck before I ravage you."

"If you think just sweet-and-sour duck will do the trick, you've got another think coming, buster. You'll have to throw in all the almond cookies."

He considered her demand. "You drive a hard bargain, Teach. Okay, the cookies are yours."

After they carried the bags into Libby's apartment, Tyler ordered her to sit down while he found plates and silverware. They sat on the floor by the coffee table, enjoying their feast by taking turns feeding each other. Tyler was even able to persuade Libby to drink more than one glass of wine.

Afterward, they leaned back against the couch with Libby ensconced in Tyler's arms. He smelled of male sweat from his work, and a hint of soap. She buried her face in his shoulder, relishing the familiarity of his embrace.

What will happen to him when I'm gone, Matthias? she silently asked.

Do you still want to go back?

I have to go back to the Tyler I grew up with. I need to see my parents, my sister and brothers. Vicki doesn't even exist here! My dad is in the hospital here and they act as if he's going to die. I can't handle it!

You know what has to be done, Libby.

She sensed his absence as soon as his words echoed in her mind.

At the same time she felt Tyler's hands slowly stroking her arms down to her wrists and back up to her shoulders. He cupped her chin with his palm and turned her face to his. His kisses were slow and drugging as she turned in his arms.

Libby held on to Tyler as if she feared she'd lose him. She worked on the buttons of his flannel shirt, wanting to feel his bare skin beneath her palms. He chuckled softly.

"I thought I was the one who was supposed to be doing the ravaging."

"You were taking too long." She unzipped his jeans and slipped her hand inside.

"Damn!" He started breathing harder. He pulled her sweater up over her head. He whistled softly when he found her wearing a delicate pink lace bra. He unhooked it and carefully folded it away from her breasts. "You are so beautiful." He nuzzled her breasts as he slowly bent her backward onto the couch cushions.

"Make love to me, Tyler," she breathed, pushing his jeans and briefs down past his hips.

He kicked them the rest of the way off as he unfastened her skirt and slid it down her legs. He found her wearing pink lace bikini panties that matched her bra. He placed his palm against the lace, feeling the warmth of her skin against his own.

"Beautiful," he murmured again, rubbing slow circles with his palm.

"I need you, Tyler." She linked her arms around his neck and pulled his face to hers. Her kisses were hungry, almost frantic with their intensity.

Tyler wanted to make slow and careful love to her. He wanted it to last forever. But he was powerless against her entreaties. He slid her panties down her legs, dropping kisses from her thighs down. He left her for a moment, then returned, thrusting deep within her.

She wrapped her legs around his hips and arched up to his driving thrust. She held on tight as if she feared he would suddenly disappear. And she cried.

Tyler felt her tears scald his skin and would have drawn back, but she wouldn't allow him to. As he felt her tighten around him, he reached down to touch the ultrasensitive bud. Libby fairly exploded around him. They shot up to the heavens together and slowly fell back.

Tyler lay with Libby nestled close to him. He could still feel her hot tears burning his skin.

"Libby?" he murmured.

She shook her head. "It was so beautiful," she whispered, turning her head and placing slow kisses on his chest. "You are my other half. You own my soul."

If any other woman had said that, Tyler would have been out the door in a flash. Except with Libby, he heard words he had been thinking. He had never felt so complete with a woman as he did with her.

"And you have mine." He moved over her and they began again what could never end between them.

It was late when Libby drove Tyler to the pre-school to pick up his truck.

"I don't like you being out so late," he told her before he left her car.

"I'll be fine," she assured him.

He touched her cheek with his fingertips as he kissed her.

"You complete me."

Chapter Seventeen

Libby was able to hold back her tears until after Tyler drove off. She had smiled at him, kissed him back and promised to see him the next evening.

Instead of driving back to her apartment, she drove to the hospital.

Libby had been a candy striper there during her high school days and knew all the back entrances. She stealthily made her way upstairs to the cardiac-care floor. She was grateful the two nurses were busy with patients and didn't see her slip into the room with Nathan Bennett's name written on the door plate.

She gulped at the sight of all the monitors and tubes.

"Daddy?" she whispered, moving forward until she reached the end of the bed. "Oh, Daddy, you were supposed to stay away from salt and all those nasty fatty foods. You were supposed to take a nice brisk walk every day. Why didn't you do it? Because I wasn't there to nag you? Please, Daddy, you can't die.''

She hovered by the side of the bed, her fingertips lightly touching his arm near the IV site. "I'm going to go back, Daddy, and get you walking every day. I'll keep you away from cheeseburgers and fries. I know now what you all tried to tell me. I wasn't alone in losing Sara. We all did. I just didn't want to give up my grief, or even share it. I can do it now, Daddy. I want to be with you all again." Her voice trembled. She backed away from the bed and made her way silently to the back stairs.

As she walked back to her car she stopped when she saw a shadow nearby. Her footsteps faltered until she realized the shadow was too small for an adult. The shadowy figure moved out into the light.

Libby gasped. "Becca? What are you doing here? Why aren't you at Mrs. Robinson's?"

"Do you believe everything now?" Becca asked, not bothering to answer Libby's questions. "Do you know you will be a good mommy?"

Libby walked up to her and dropped down on one knee. She ignored the cold ground beneath her.

"Who are you really?" She could barely voice the question.

Becca smiled. "You know." She leaned forward, kissing her on the cheek. With a butterfly touch, she closed Libby's eyes.

When she opened them Becca was gone. Libby stood up and looked around.

"Becca?" She called out the name, although she didn't expect an answer.

Libby didn't waste any time after that. She jumped in her car, but instead of heading for her apartment, drove to the park where it had all begun. She got out of her car and walked over to the swings.

"Matthias!" She spun around. "Matthias, come out now!"

He appeared with a long-suffering expression on his face.

"Do you realize what time it is?"

She ignored his question. "I want to go on with my life. I want to apologize to Tyler for ignoring his pain all these months. For not allowing us to comfort each other. I want to make sure my dad stays on the right track for his health. I want to renew my relationship with my mother. I want it all the way it should be. And—" she choked "—and I want to be back there so Tyler and I can have another child. Sara would want that." Tears ran down her cheeks.

Matthias's normally stern features softened in a smile.

"You're willing to have love back in your life again?"

She nodded.

"It's always been there, Libby. You just had to take hold of it again."

The moment his words were spoken, he disappeared. Libby blinked against the snowflakes swirling around her face until she couldn't see.

"Wait!" she cried out.

Just as quickly, the snowflakes were gone.

"Libby!"

She spun around at the sound of the familiar voice.

"Tyler?"

He ran toward her and hugged her tightly. "What were you trying to do? Scare the hell out of me? I'm sorry we did what we did without talking to you first, but—"

She quickly pressed her fingertips against his mouth to silence him. She noticed she now wore her ring and nearly wept at the comfortable pressure of it against her finger.

"I wouldn't have listened," she told him. "I've been so wrong, Tyler. I walled myself off from everyone, when I needed you so badly. I love you so much." She peppered his face with kisses. "I don't want to lose you, Tyler."

He looked stunned by her announcement. "Sweetheart, you wouldn't have lost me. I love you too much to ever leave you. You complete me.''

The simple emotion in those words, words she'd heard once before, made her realize that she hadn't left the other Tyler behind. He was here, and she was now able to appreciate how precious he was. How precious this second chance at mending their relationship was.

She started crying. ''I want us to start over. I want us to have another baby.''

Tyler stiffened in her arms. ''Are you sure?'' He looked as if he couldn't believe what he was hearing.

Libby nodded. ''Can we go home now?'' she pleaded. ''I need to be home.''

Tyler kept his arms wrapped around her as they walked toward his truck.

It didn't take him long to realize her tears were of joy. He wasn't sure why. He wasn't sure what had brought about this change in Libby, but he was going to rejoice in it. His old Libby was back, and he would be thankful for it every day of his life.

Christmas, one year later

''I DON'T THINK there're enough lights,'' Libby said, looking at a house that appeared to be made of lights.

"Honey, there's no room for anymore lights." Tyler pulled off his gloves, looking like a long-suffering husband. "Aren't you freezing out here?"

Libby wore only a white, long-sleeved blouse and a red-and-green-print ankle-length jumper. Tiny Christmas decorations and Santas and snow-men made up the print. Her hair was pulled back on one side with a red velvet bow that held a spring of mistletoe.

"All right," she decided, "but I still think we could have more lights." She followed him back into the house.

As they entered, a squeal from the living room caught their attention.

"There they are, lovey," Vicki cooed, holding up a baby in a red velvet dress with a red ribbon around her head.

"My darling!" Libby took her out of Vicki's arms. "Did your aunt Vicki show you the Christmas tree?"

"Did your aunt Vicki explain she can never take you shopping?" Tyler inserted, dropping a kiss on the baby's head. She looked up at the sound of her daddy's voice and waved her arms.

He looked past the baby to Libby's shining face. He'd almost feared her words a year ago were temporary, but they hadn't been. She had called the entire family together and apologized to them all for keeping back from them. She'd said she knew it wouldn't be easy, but she hoped they would all help her. Tears had flowed freely, and that had been the beginning. Libby seemed to enjoy making sure her father stayed on his special diet and she took walks with him every day. She contacted Miss Regina and for now was substitute teaching at the preschool. But the biggest change was her relationship with Tyler.

She seduced him. She entranced him so that he couldn't imagine ever spending time with another woman. Their latest joy was the child Libby held in her arms. Two months ago, he had cried with Libby as their baby came into the world. While the fear lingered in their minds that tragedy might strike twice, they didn't allow it to interfere in their joy.

"Hey, lady, you're under the mistletoe," he whispered, tilting Libby's chin up with his fingers. His kiss was far from light and promised much more later.

"Excuse me, but are you sure a child should be present during such debauchery?" Vicki teased, taking the baby from Libby. "Can't you two keep your hands off each other?"

"We don't want to." Libby smiled at her sister. She turned back to her husband. "But I guess we will have to behave while the rest of the family is here."

Tyler kissed her again. "All right, but I will demand all your attention after they leave."

"You got it."

Libby smiled as the faint sound of a bell tinkled overhead.

Tyler frowned. "What was that?"

She looked at the brightly lit tree with piles of gaily wrapped gifts underneath. Garlands and tiny lights were everywhere and the scent of pine filled the air.

"That was the sound of an entity getting his wings," she murmured, pulling her husband back to her.

Vicki shook her head in amusement at her sister and brother-in-law's obvious desire for each other. She headed for the kitchen, where the warm smells of baked goods abounded.

"Come on, Becca. You're way too young to see this."

Epilogue

"I must say it was a job well done," Matthias announced to the Council of Elders.

"Yes, Matthias, we are very pleased with your success with Elizabeth Barnes," Simon replied. "In fact, we are so pleased, we feel there is only one reward that would equal such a triumph."

Matthias wanted to shout with glee, but if he was to be a member of the Council of Elders, he knew he would have to be more circumspect. Instead, he stood there, a model of dignified reserve, waiting to hear them tell him he was now a member.

Simon kept smiling. "What we bestow on you is only right, Matthias. And in time, I am sure you will agree with us. Your next assignment will be your most challenging yet."

Matthias's eyes widened with shock as he realized their intent.

"*No!*"

A HOLIDAY RECIPE FROM THE KITCHEN OF
Linda Wisdom

Every year, the Saturday before Christmas, we have
friends and family over. The men usually
stay in one room talking. The women usually stay
around the food. And the kids are all upstairs playing
Nintendo or watching TV, knowing only blood drawn will
lose their playing privileges. This cheesecake is just one
of the goodies offered.

PUMPKIN CHEESECAKE

Crust: 1/2 cup gingersnap crumbs

Filling: 2 lbs cream cheese, softened

1 1/2 cups sugar	1/3 cup all-purpose flour, sifted
1 1/2 tsp cinnamon	1 tsp nutmeg
1 tsp ground cloves	1/4 tsp allspice
1/8 tsp salt	6 eggs
	2 cups pumpkin

Topping: 1 cup heavy cream
1/2 cup chopped pecans (optional)

Sprinkle the gingersnap crumbs on the sides of a well-buttered springform pan. Chill in refrigerator.

Beat together all the filling ingredients—except the pumpkin—until very smooth. Add the pumpkin and beat until mixed. Pour the mixture into chilled springform pan and bake in preheated 325°F oven for 1 1/2 hours. Turn off the oven and let the cheesecake stay in the open oven for 30 minutes. Then remove and let cool on a wire rack. Carefully remove the sides of the pan.

Topping: Whip the heavy cream until stiff peaks form, and spread over the top of the cake. Sprinkle with pecans.

Take 4 bestselling love stories FREE

Plus get a FREE surprise gift!

Special Limited-time Offer

Mail to Harlequin Reader Service®

3010 Walden Avenue
P.O. Box 1867
Buffalo, N.Y. 14240-1867

YES! Please send me 4 free Harlequin American Romance® novels and my free surprise gift. Then send me 4 brand-new novels every month, which I will receive months before they appear in bookstores. Bill me at the low price of $3.12 each plus 25¢ delivery and applicable sales tax, if any.* That's the complete price and a savings of over 10% off the cover prices—quite a bargain! I understand that accepting the books and gift places me under no obligation ever to buy any books. I can always return a shipment and cancel at any time. Even if I never buy another book from Harlequin, the 4 free books and the surprise gift are mine to keep forever.

154 BPA A3UM

Name	(PLEASE PRINT)	
Address		Apt. No.
City	State	Zip

This offer is limited to one order per household and not valid to present Harlequin American Romance® subscribers. *Terms and prices are subject to change without notice. Sales tax applicable in N.Y.

UAM-696   ©1990 Harlequin Enterprises Limited

WELCOME TO *Love Inspired* ™

A brand-new series of contemporary inspirational love stories.

Join men and women as they learn valuable lessons about facing the challenges of today's world and about life, love and faith.

Look for:

Christmas Rose
by Lacey Springer

A Matter of Trust
by Cheryl Wolverton

The Wedding Quilt
by Lenora Worth

Available in retail outlets
in November 1997.

LIFT YOUR SPIRITS AND GLADDEN YOUR HEART with *Love Inspired* ™!

Steeple
Hill™

Free Gift Offer

With a Free Gift proof-of-purchase
from any Harlequin® book, you can receive
a beautiful cubic zirconia pendant.

This stunning marquise-shaped stone is a genuine cubic
zirconia—accented by an 18" gold tone necklace.
(Approximate retail value $19.95)

Send for yours today...
compliments of HARLEQUIN®

To receive your free gift, a cubic zirconia pendant, send us one original proof-of-purchase, photocopies not accepted, from the back of any Harlequin Romance®, Harlequin Presents®, Harlequin Temptation®, Harlequin Superromance®, Harlequin Intrigue®, Harlequin American Romance®, or Harlequin Historicals® title available at your favorite retail outlet, together with the Free Gift Certificate, plus a check or money order for $1.65 u.s./$2.15 can. (do not send cash) to cover postage and handling, payable to Harlequin Free Gift Offer. We will send you the specified gift. Allow 6 to 8 weeks for delivery. Offer good until December 31, 1997, or while quantities last. Offer valid in the U.S. and Canada only.

Free Gift Certificate

Name: _____

Address: _____

City: _____ State/Province: _____ Zip/Postal Code: _____

Mail this certificate, one proof-of-purchase and a check or money order for postage and handling to: HARLEQUIN FREE GIFT OFFER 1997. In the U.S.: 3010 Walden Avenue, P.O. Box 9071, Buffalo NY 14269-9057. In Canada: P.O. Box 604, Fort Erie, Ontario L2Z 5X3.

FREE GIFT OFFER　　　　　　　　　　　**084-KEZ**

ONE PROOF-OF-PURCHASE
To collect your fabulous FREE GIFT, a cubic zirconia pendant, you must include this original proof-of-purchase for each gift with the properly completed Free Gift Certificate.

084-KEZR

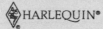